SHE'S GONE

A PSYCHOLOGICAL THRILLER- FEATURING DI
SAM COBBS

M A COMLEY

ACKNOWLEDGMENTS

Thank you as always to my rock, Jean, I'd be lost without
you in my life.

Special thanks as always go to @studioenp for their superb cover
design expertise.

My heartfelt thanks go to my wonderful editor Abby, my proofreaders
Joseph, Barbara and Jacqueline for spotting all the lingering nits.

Thank you also to my amazing ARC group who help to keep me sane
during this process.

And a special thanks to Dee for beta reading this novel for me.

To Mary, gone, but never forgotten. I hope you found the peace you
were searching for my dear friend.

ALSO BY M A COMLEY

Grave Intention (Intention series #2)

Devious Intention (Intention #3)

Merry Widow (A Lorne Simpkins short story)

It's A Dog's Life (A Lorne Simpkins short story)

Cozy Mystery Series

Murder at the Wedding

Murder at the Hotel

Murder by the Sea

Death on the Coast

Death By Association

A Time To Heal (A Sweet Romance)

A Time For Change (A Sweet Romance)

High Spirits

The Temptation series (Romantic Suspense/New Adult Novellas)

Past Temptation

Lost Temptation

1

"*D*addy, let's sing it again."

Martin glanced sideways at Louise, the new love of his life, then looked in the rear-view mirror and smiled at his adorable five-year-old daughter. "Darling, we've already sung it ten times. Why don't we let someone else choose a song instead, eh?"

Adele stared at her father and pouted. She swiftly turned her head to look out of the window at the passing scenery—The Lake District in all its finery and an abundance of vivid landscapes, which they intended to explore over the coming week, were on show ahead of them.

Martin had his little girl back with him after months of battling her mother, Deborah, through the family court system. He had to prove he was willing to give his daughter the attention she deserved, instead of ploughing all his devotion into his newly formed family. It was all nonsense; Deborah had sullied his name during their mind-numbing trips to court. He was a far better person than she'd portrayed him to be. He loved his daughter, more than life itself at times.

When none of the children could come up with a suitable song to sing, he asked, "Come on, kids, we're almost at our destination, tell us what *you* want to do during the holiday. We're open to suggestions."

"Play football in the park," Jake was quick to shout.

Martin laughed. "Hey, that's a given, mate. What about you, Matilda and Adele, is there anything in particular you girls want to do?"

Adele's pout deepened, which upset him. He swallowed down the twinge of hurt which had surfaced, not allowing her to see she had won. In that respect, she was the opposite of her mother who was usually easy-going. Matilda, on the other hand, beamed and said, "Beach! I want to build lots of sandcastles with the sand."

"Again, that's something high up on our agenda. Adele, what about you, honey?"

"I don't care. Do whatever."

Louise's hand squeezed his thigh. He faced her, keeping one eye on the winding road ahead of them. "Let her be, we'll sort something out during the course of the week."

"Okay, here we go, kids. We're climbing now. I think this song will be appropriate, join in if you know it." He winked. "She'll be coming around the mountain when she comes."

He quickly looked in the rear-view mirror. The children were all staring at him, as if he was singing in a foreign language. Louise burst out laughing. "You're kidding me. That's as old as the damn hills surrounding us."

He turned to her and shrugged. "It's the best I could come up with in the circumstances. At least, it made you laugh. Hey, do me a favour, you try and think of something more suitable, then."

"That's easy, we're all going on a summer holiday…"

He glanced in his mirror at the back seat and all the kids were swaying and singing along. All right, some of the words were out of place or perhaps missing, but at least they joined in. Not for the first time, he was grateful to have in his life who he had come to cherish and love over the past few months. He couldn't imagine his life without her steadying and loving influence.

He rounded the corner at the top of the steep hill and everyone gasped. He spotted a lay-by up ahead and decided to pull over to admire the breathtaking view.

"Wow, it's even better than I remembered," Louise said in a hushed voice. She seemed mesmerised by the scenery ahead and all around them.

"I'm really disappointed," Martin muttered.

Louise's head snapped around to face him. "What? Are you crazy?"

He grinned at the horrified expression distorting her beautiful face. "If you'll let me finish, I was about to say, I'm really disappointed I've never ventured up this way for a holiday before. It's magical. Spellbinding. I'd even go as far as referring to it as hypnotic. Or would that be going over the top in my appraisal?"

"No, I think you've got it just right. I've been coming up here for years with my parents and the view never fails to impress." Louise peered over her shoulder at the children. "What do you think, guys?"

"It's wonderful, Mummy. I want to climb every mountain, can we do that?" Jake asked enthusiastically, rubbing his hands together.

Martin chuckled. "It would probably take us all week to climb one, let alone all of them. But it'll be an incentive to visit the area again later on in the year, won't it, pal?"

"Yay, I was hoping you'd say that. Coolio, I'd be up for it. What about you, Matty?"

Matilda seemed a little distracted, too awestruck by the view to reply. After her brother dug her in the ribs, she said, "Yes, I'd love that. Magical, isn't it, Adele?"

Adele stared out of the side window, her mouth gaping open. She leaned forward in her seat a little to gain a better view past Jake and Matilda. "It's wonderful. Thank you for bringing me, Daddy."

His hard heart softened. Every time she uttered the word *Daddy*, she significantly melted his insides. He'd missed his daughter so much. Life wasn't the same without seeing her every day. Deborah had known that, and he predicted it was why she'd insisted on dragging him through the court. Like most women in a marriage breakdown, she had the upper hand regarding the children's welfare. The court failed willing fathers most of the time; always siding with the mothers, discounting any feelings the father may have and ditching a father's

3

abilities to care for a child, in favour of giving the primary custody to the mother. Most of the time that was a good idea, but there were occasions when the law was an arse, and something serious happened to the child in the wake of such a decision.

He had never faulted Deborah's capabilities in caring for his daughter, not one iota, but there was an underlying niggle within him that she sat at home every night, virtually twisting the knife in his back, making Adele wary of him. As she'd proven so far on the trip. He had to set that aside for now. Concentrate on the here and now, appreciate the fact that Louise and her two children had welcomed him into their home after knowing him for less than a year. His life had been enriched beyond anything he could have imagined, since he'd met Louise.

This trip wasn't just about getting away from it all, no, Martin had every intention of going down on one knee to pop the question, this evening, if the opportunity presented itself, maybe after the kids had gone to bed.

"Are you all right, love? You seem a bit distant," Louise whispered.

He smiled and leaned over to kiss her. "Enjoying being here with you guys, as a family. Thinking how lucky I am right now." A flock of swallows darted past the vehicle.

"You're such a softie. Come on, let's go, we've still got half an hour's drive before we find the cottage. I hope I can remember the way."

"You will. You've never let me down yet."

"Charmer. Hey, there's always a first time."

The engine started up, cutting through the magical experience they had all encountered. "The final leg now, kids. Shout out when you can see the highest sheep up on the hills, okay?"

The game kept the kids amused until Louise pointed at the road they needed to take up ahead. "It's that one, I'm sure it is. It's quite narrow, but that means we won't get disturbed by any traffic passing by, plus I thought it would be an ideal place for the kids to play."

"Okay, let's see if we can find this cottage." Martin indicated right and began the climb up the small hill. As they reached the top, there stood an old stone cottage.

"Yes, I was right. That's it. Isn't it adorable?" Louise gushed, her face lit up with excitement.

"It sure is. One question. Is it really big enough to take the five of us?"

Louise sniggered. "Of course it is. I wouldn't have booked it otherwise."

"Fair enough." He pulled up outside the front of the cottage and unlocked the doors. The kids bolted from the car as soon as they saw the swing and slide in the back garden. "Don't go wandering off. Stay right there until we've unloaded the car, got that?"

"Yes, Daddy," Adele shouted back, her demeanour changing in an instant to what it had been like in the car.

He sighed and watched the kids playing for a second or two. Louise slipped her arms around his middle and rested her head on his back. "They're going to have a blast. My two love Adele already."

"I hope you're right. Thanks for inviting her along, it meant the world to me."

"Hey, we're a family, buster, whether you like it or not; and that includes Adele. Come on, let's get this lot inside. You take the cases and I'll ferry the groceries in."

"About that... why bring so much? We'll be eating out most days, won't we?"

"You've clearly never been around three kids before, they're constant grazers from the minute they wake up to the time they go to bed."

"No way! Why aren't they the size of this cottage then?"

"Because I don't allow them to sit in front of the TV all day, playing computer games. I make sure they burn off all that excess energy and calories. We'll probably need to top up the cupboards again before the week is out, too."

He shook his head. "I had no idea. Maybe I'm doing Deborah an injustice then, she's always begging me for more maintenance for Adele."

Louise shrugged. "It's always easier to feed an extra adult than a child, in my experience anyway, especially if the child turns out to be a fussy eater. What's Adele like?"

"Pass. Out of practice, I'm ashamed to say. I've never really been around at mealtime. I've always worked exceptionally long hours, which meant I missed out on the adventure of mealtimes and having to feed a five-year-old."

"It's okay. We'll play it by ear then."

They began to ferry the cases, overnight bags and carrier bags full of shopping into the tiny cottage.

"What do you think of upstairs?" Louise asked, packing the tins of baked beans into one of the lower cupboards in the quaint galley kitchen, which was characterful with a flagstone floor and an exposed stone wall at the rear.

"It's as small upstairs as it is down here. I suppose we'll be out most of the time and we only sleep in the bedroom, don't we?"

Louise straightened with a twinkle in her eye. "If you say so. I was hoping for more this week, but I'll go with the flow."

He grabbed her and kissed her deeply. "I meant... the kids will only be sleeping, not us. This week, I intend showing you just how much you mean to me, every which way possible."

"I think I know how much you love me, there's no need for you to go the extra mile on my account."

He released her and glanced over her shoulder. "Get you. Are you all done in here?"

"Not quite, one more bag to go. Why don't you check on the kids? Do me a favour, discreetly inspect the fence and make sure it's intact while you're out there. The last thing we need is one of the kids attempting to explore the surroundings on their own."

"I was just about to do it. Great minds. Join us when you can."

"I will. Want a coffee?"

"I thought you'd never ask." He ducked out of the way with a chuckle, doing his best to dodge her playful slap.

"Hmm... I'll make up a jug of squash for the kids. I won't be long."

When he ventured outside, the children were all playing happily together. "Having fun, everyone?"

"The greatest time ever, Daddy," Adele replied.

"It's all right," Jake said. "When can we go out and start exploring?"

"What? Aren't you tired after the trip?"

"No, I'm buzzing. I can't wait to begin our adventure."

Martin ruffled the eight-year-old's hair. He'd taken to the boy the first time he'd laid eyes on him. Jake had welcomed Martin into the fold too, eager to have a father figure around after spending four years alone with his sister and mother since his father had upped and left.

Louise had done a marvellous job of working full time while raising two small children, that's what he admired most about her. She could have crumbled the day her ex-husband, Chris, had walked out on her, but she hadn't. Instead, she'd asked her parents to help out with child-care and thrown herself into work, knowing that the house could have been taken from her if she hadn't kept up the mortgage payments on it. Her parents, Anne and Tony, had recently both retired from the army and had settled near Louise after years of travelling the globe with the military. It hadn't taken them long to adjust, not with having Jake and Matilda around. It had turned out to be a win-win situation for all concerned. Even more so when Martin had walked into Louise's life.

He watched the children playing happily together, his mind flitting back to their first meeting. Martin was a sales manager for an export and import firm and had advertised in the local paper for a new secretary. There had been five successful candidates who had got past the first stage and whom he'd invited for an interview. Out of those five, two hadn't said a word throughout the interview other than answered his questions with a clipped response; they had instantly been relegated to the 'not suitable' pile. The other three all had something about them, but at the end of the day, it had been Louise who had stood out. Her experience was superior to the others, and she had a great personality to boot, ensuring she sparkled on the day. An added bonus was that she had been the most attractive of the interviewees, too.

Since his own relationship had been faltering for some years, it hadn't taken him long before he'd confided in Louise about his disastrous marriage with Deborah. One drink led to another; and before long, they'd started an affair at work. Not something he was proud of; however, Louise had turned out to be everything Deborah wasn't—supportive, caring, enthusiastic about his work. There was no doubt Deborah was a great mother; that had never been in dispute in his eyes, but he regarded Louise as the whole package. Bright, attentive, loving, adored by her children. The perfect all-round mother and definitely wife material. All he needed now was to pop the question and wait patiently for the divorce to come through to end their six-year marriage.

He'd always felt trapped with Debs; whether it was the truth or just his perspective on their relationship, he wasn't sure. It had been full on from the first week, really. Lust had seen to that. The second month into their relationship, she'd announced that she had missed her period and thought she was pregnant.

They had carried out the test in the en suite bathroom together. Mixed emotions ran through him when the test proved positive. On the one hand, he was joyous that his sperm had done their thing to create a tiny human being, but on the other hand, their relationship had only just begun. Still, Martin was a man of honour, to a point; he knew he could never walk out on Debs, knew he had to step up to the plate, and he did so, willingly. But after only a few months, Deb's personality had altered significantly towards him. At the time, he accepted it was par for the course, what with a woman's hormones being all over the place during pregnancy. However, after Adele was born, Deb's attitude got worse instead of better. She'd given up her job as a shop assistant, insisting she was tired and couldn't stand to be on her feet all day. At first, Martin had accepted that as an excuse—he wasn't a heartless and uncaring man at all. Once Adele was six months old, though, he started dropping the odd hint about when she was going to return to work. Pinpointing it, that's when he realised Debs had trapped him; she saw him as a man to meet all her needs without having to give anything in return, at least in his eyes.

Louise snuck up behind him and placed her arms around his waist. "You were miles away."

He pulled her to the side of him, kissed her on the cheek and rested his head against hers. "I was. Sorry, did you call out?"

"I did, it doesn't matter. Anything wrong?"

"No, not really. Just standing here... thinking." He smiled down at her.

"About anything in particular?"

"Yes and no. I'll tell you later. Shall we fix some dinner?"

"You read my mind. I bet everyone is hungry after their trip. I've got a cooked chicken. I thought I'd prepare a salad, if that's okay?"

"Sounds ideal. You're amazing."

Louise laughed. "It's only chicken and a salad, hardly *MasterChef* standard."

"I wasn't referring to the food and you know it."

Louise smiled. "I'll make a start, you can round the kids up; give me ten minutes to sort out the chicken first, if you will?"

"I feel guilty, you being lumbered with organising the dinner. Why don't I come inside and help you? This is your holiday as well, sweetheart."

"I know it is, but you drove us here, now it's my turn to look after you. No arguments."

They shared a lingering kiss, and Louise went back inside the cottage. Martin, putting his bout of reflectiveness behind him, where it belonged, joined the children. Adele was on the swing, her head down, swinging gently in the breeze. He stood behind her. "Want a push, sweetie?"

His daughter glanced over her shoulder and smiled. "Yes please, Daddy. I want to go high."

"Then high you shall go, my beautiful princess."

He pulled the seat backwards and let it go. Once the momentum kicked in, he pushed Adele harder each time until she was screaming with joy. *Oh, how I've missed having you in my life over the past eight to nine months. You'll never know how much I love you, munchkin.*

9

He slowed the swing down. "Come on then, let's go and have something to eat. Louise has kindly fixed us a lovely meal."

"I'm not hungry. I want to play out here!" Adele shouted, the angry retort attached to a full-on pout.

Martin groaned internally, but did his best to keep his smile intact. "There will be plenty of playtime ahead of us this week. You must be hungry after that long trip, darling. Come on, down you get." He held out his hand for her to take.

Adele hopped off the swing, ignored his outstretched hand and stomped ahead of him. She entered the house and slammed the door behind her. *Yep, just like your damn mother. Stubborn and without compromise.*

With a sunken heart, he called for Matilda and Jake to join him. They were good kids and came to stand beside him within seconds. "Let's go see what's for dinner, shall we?"

"I'd like that," Matilda replied. She slipped a tiny hand into his and tugged him towards the house. Jake ran on ahead of them. "What's wrong with Adele? Doesn't she like you, Martin?"

The words stung and ripped at his insides. Despite the devastation running through him, he smiled down at Matilda. "She'll be fine after a few days. I guess all this is a huge adjustment for her."

"Ah, she's not used to you being around, is she?"

"No, through no fault of my own, that's right, love. It'll take her a while, but I'm sure if we're all nice to her, it'll help her adjust quicker. What do you say?"

"I agree. I want her to be my new bestest friend."

Martin halted and crouched down beside her. "That would be wonderful; it would make all this so much easier on her, on all of us, if that were to happen."

She shrugged her little shoulders and said, "I don't think she wants to be my friend."

"I'm sure that's not the case, sweetie. What makes you say that?"

"The look she gives me and Jake." Matilda shuddered.

Martin hugged her to him. "Aww... I think all this is proving too much for her. I don't think she means it, sweetheart."

"Okay." Matilda slipped out of his arms and ran into the house.

Martin stood, inhaled a lungful of the clear fresh air and followed her through the front door where he found Louise carrying the serving dishes to the table. "Here, let me take those."

"I'm fine. You wash up and see how Adele is getting on. She's been upstairs for a while now."

He rolled his eyes and took the narrow stairs two at a time. At the top he turned left and knocked gently on the bathroom door. "Adele, are you in there, honey?"

There was no response. He strained an ear, but heard nothing for a few seconds until he caught a faint sniffle. He closed his eyes, hoping to push down the panic beginning to rise. "Darling, open the door for Daddy, be a good girl now."

The door remained closed. It suddenly dawned on him that he was out of his depth. *How would you deal with a child who wasn't prepared to join in? Who refused to speak to you, tell you what the problem was?* In truth, he didn't have a clue. He'd never had to deal with her mood swings because, ashamedly, he'd rarely spent any time with her since her birth. Even when he and Debs had been loved up after Adele was born, he'd worked extra hours during the week, and often at the weekend, to replace the income Debs had lost by refusing to entertain going back to work.

Another sniffle sounded. He tapped on the door again. "Adele, please speak to me. Aren't you having fun, love? Do you want to go back home?" He winced as the words tripped out.

Silence.

"Adele, open the door. Let's talk about this."

Again, nothing.

Until finally, the small bolt slid back and his daughter opened the door. He pushed it back to reveal an upset child which was killing him inside.

He crouched down to her level and held out his arms. "Come here. Daddy needs a cuddle."

Adele gingerly walked into his arms, placed her head on his

shoulder and whispered, "I don't know what to do, Daddy. I don't know you."

Tears instantly welled, and a huge lump developed in his throat. *What in God's name am I supposed to say to that?*

Finally, he cleared his throat and said, "I know. That's my fault, sweetie. Let's see if we can change that over the coming week. Would you like to try?"

"I think so. I miss Mummy. Can she come and stay with us?"

"Mummy is busy, honey. She told me you could spend the week with us, having fun. I'll tell you what, if the weather is good tomorrow, we'll go down to the beach; you'd like that, feeling the sand between your toes, wouldn't you?"

"What's sand? I've never been to the beach."

"You'll see tomorrow. You'll love it, I promise you with all my heart. Now, are you hungry?"

She inhaled a shuddering breath. "I think so. Can I have a cheese sandwich?"

"Try and eat the dinner Louise has prepared for you first. If you don't like it, then we'll make you a cheese sandwich."

"I'll try."

He stood and clutched her hand tightly, then led her back down the stairs and into the living room, to the small dining table squeezed under the stairs.

"Everything all right?" Louise frowned in concern.

"I think so. Adele is missing her mummy."

"Aww… you're allowed to miss her, sweetie. Come and sit next to Matilda."

Adele shook her head and gripped her father's hand tighter. "I want to sit with my daddy."

The only problem was, that seat was occupied by Jake. Louise and Martin glanced at each other. Eventually, Louise said, "Jake, sorry, love, would you mind moving seats?"

"Do I have to?" Jake shovelled an extra portion of chicken into his mouth.

"No, but you'd be doing me a favour if you did."

"All right, just for you, Mum. Can I get an extra portion of pudding?"

Louise and Martin both laughed. "Yes, son, you can." Louise leaned over and pecked her son on the cheek. "Thank you."

Once Jake had moved seats, Martin lifted Adele and placed her on the chair, then tucked it under the table. He sat down next to his daughter and loaded both of their plates with chicken and salad.

Adele stared at her plate for a long time, then she picked at the chicken but left the salad.

"Don't you like salad, Adele?" Louise asked gently.

"I don't know, I've never eaten it. It doesn't look nice. We have a rabbit at playschool who eats that." She pointed at the lettuce.

Martin eyed Louise over the top of his daughter's head and shrugged.

"You can leave it if you try and don't like the taste," Louise assured her.

Adele stuck her fork into the chicken slices and raised a large one to her mouth. Once she'd tasted it and found she liked it, she dug her fork into the next slice until all the chicken had gone.

"Try a tomato, sweetie," Martin urged, pointing out the red fruit on her plate.

She tried to puncture the skin with her fork and the small cherry tomato shot off her plate and onto the table. They all roared with laughter, even Adele.

"Want to try that again?" Martin asked. He returned the tomato to his daughter's plate and using her fork, he speared it and offered it up for her to eat.

She hesitated for a while and then opened her tiny mouth to consume the fruit.

"There, did you like it?" Louise asked.

"Yes, I think so. I don't want anything else. I'm full." Adele sat back, folded her arms and pursed her lips tightly, blocking any attempt of Martin trying to force-feed her.

Louise shook her head, telling him not to push her too much.

Instead, the four of them continued to enjoy their dinner and left Adele to sulk.

After clearing the plates and depositing them in the kitchen, Louise returned with a shop-bought trifle. "Who's for pudding?"

Matilda and Jake excitedly raised their hands and squealed in delight. But Adele remained aloof and shook her head. "Don't like it."

"What? Since when doesn't a child eat trifle?" Martin replied in mock-disbelief.

"It's fine," Louise muttered. "How about a piece of fruit instead, Adele?"

"I want ice cream," Adele snapped back.

"Ah, well, I knew it wouldn't last on the journey here so I didn't bother buying any, we'll buy some tomorrow to put in the freezer, how's that?"

Adele glared at Louise and shouted, "I want it *now*."

Martin's fist slammed on the table, startling everyone. "That's enough. I think it's time you learnt some manners, my girl. Louise has created this lovely meal for you which you've barely touched and…"

Louise shook her head, making him pause. "It's okay, Martin, all this is new to Adele. She must be tired after her long journey."

Adele's head swivelled between Louise and Martin as though she was watching a game of tennis at Wimbledon.

Nothing more was said as the four of them tucked into their luscious trifle. Martin tried to offer Adele a spoonful, but she stubbornly turned her head and clamped her lips together.

After dinner, they cleared the plates. Louise insisted on doing the washing-up while Martin occupied the children with a game of Snap. At last, Adele appeared to perk up. She even won a few times, which put an extra smile on her chubby little face.

Bath time came around not long after. Matilda and Jake shared a bath, but Adele refused to, which didn't surprise Martin one bit. Instead, she agreed to take a shower and Louise stood in the bathroom, acting as a chaperone for the five-year-old. After which, Martin took over. All the kids shared the main bedroom. There was a double bed and a single tucked into the eaves. Matilda and Adele shared the double while Jake hopped into the single. Martin read them a bedtime story about the Gruffalo. All three of them listened intently. Now and then, either Matilda or Jake interrupted Martin to ask a question, but again, Adele said nothing, she just stared up at the ceiling, waiting for him to continue.

The final words read, he slapped the book shut and kissed the three of them goodnight. Matilda's and Jake's eyes were already drooping, but Adele still appeared to be wide awake. He stretched out beside his daughter and cuddled her. At first, she was as stiff as a board. He sang her the soothing lullaby he used to sing right after she was born, and eventually, after around an hour, she drifted off to sleep.

Lifting her head, he slipped his arm out and kissed her on the forehead. *You're such an angelic soul when you're asleep. I hope you're not going to make us regret bringing you here this week.*

After checking on Matilda and Jake, ensuring they were both warm and covered by the quilt, he tiptoed out of the room and back downstairs where he found Louise enjoying a glass of wine and watching *Emmerdale*. She switched off the TV, knowing how much he detested the soaps.

"All asleep, finally?"

He nodded and sipped at his glass of wine. "Yep, I don't have to tell you who was the last to drop off, do I?"

Louise giggled and snuggled up to him. She placed the woollen rug over his lap. "This place is lovely, but chilly in the evening; that's the trouble when you have all these exposed walls. Not worth lighting the wood burner though, we'll be off to bed ourselves soon, right?"

"If you insist. Are you having fun?"

"The best time ever. I hope Adele settles down soon and begins to enjoy herself."

His arm tightened around her. "That's what I'm hoping, too. Is it just me or does she treat me like a stranger most of the time? I know she calls me Daddy, but that could be just a word to her, one without a meaning attached."

Louise pulled away from him and sat upright. "I think you're guilty of overthinking things. You *are* her daddy, no one in this world can dispute that fact."

"I know..." He waved a hand. "Just ignore me, foolish words circulating my head, that's all. We've had a long trip today, I suppose it has taken its toll on all of us, in one way or another."

"It has. It's always better to look on the positive side in such situations."

He pulled her close again and rested his chin on the top of her head, inhaling the essence of the tropical shampoo she loved to use. "It's just... after not seeing her in months, I feel like she's forgotten my role in her life."

"Give her time to adjust. Let's be fair, we don't really know what her mother has been saying about you. You know how vindictive exes can be."

"You think she'd do that? Debs always used to have a vicious tongue in her head, but to purposefully set out to destroy my good name as a father, in my own daughter's eyes, even for her, that would be below the belt."

"Let's keep a close eye on the situation and make sure it doesn't get out of hand. Maybe she'll be entirely different in the morning. Give her a chance to get used to having Matilda and Jake around. That's four new people she needs to find her feet with, imagine being in her shoes."

"That's why I love you so much. Because your heart is large enough to care about everyone and their needs."

Louise angled her head up to his. He planted a kiss on her lips that went on for a few minutes, dousing the concerns rattling around in his head. After they parted, he threw the rug aside, stood and held out a hand for her to take.

"Let's go and see how comfortable the bed is, shall we?"

Louise slipped her hand into his, brushed her lips across his cheek and said, "Lead the way, I'm all yours."

2

"*R*ight, kids, let's go! Time is running out fast on this holiday. I don't want to waste another minute in this cottage when we can be out there exploring. Who's with me?" Martin shouted from the bottom of the stairs the next morning. He glanced at the clock on the kitchen wall—it was nine-thirty already.

The children had all been dressed for hours; Matilda and Jake were used to rising early anyway, but Adele had surprised him when she ran down the stairs behind them, eager for breakfast.

They'd all tucked into a bowl of Shreddies, followed by a mountain of toast between them while Martin and Louise settled on a bacon sandwich.

After bolting down their breakfast, the kids had chased each other back up the stairs again. Martin watched the miraculous change in his daughter with a light heart.

Louise slipped her arms around his waist. "Didn't I tell you that you were worrying about nothing?"

"You did. Shall we both get them dressed or how do you want to play it?"

"They should be capable of dressing themselves, washing or showering is a different matter though. I'll go and organise them."

"Anything specific you want me to do?"

"I brought a bunch of picnic stuff with us, you can have a root around in the fridge and decide what to take on our trip today. I would avoid making any sandwiches as we've had bread for breakfast."

He sipped at his drink. "Too many carbs, right? See, I'm learning fast, living with you."

"It's better to start them off early in this life. Adapting to change once they've been used to stodge will only be more difficult further down the line."

"You're such a wonderful mother and I'm a very lucky person to have you in my life."

"You are." She chuckled. "I'm off. I know you're eager to get out there."

"It's our holiday as well as theirs and I intend to enjoy every waking moment of it."

Louise left him to it. He wandered back into the kitchen, tidied away the breakfast dishes that Louise had already washed up and opened the fridge door to examine the contents. It was loaded with delicious goodies, most of them healthy options, but he spotted there were a few stray items in there as well. He grinned when he spied the Melton Mowbray pork pies, his personal favourite brand. She was such a thoughtful person.

He gathered the collection of salad vegetables from the crisper and set about washing it all and chopping it up into bite-sized pieces. *Hmm... all I need now is a container to put it all in.* He searched the few cupboards in the small kitchen, but couldn't find a Tupperware box or anything that would possibly fit the bill. In the end, he resorted to using a roll of plastic bags for each of the individual ingredients. "It'll have to do."

By the time he'd shoved all the prepared food into a spare carrier bag, the rest of the family were ready. He added a bottle of lemonade and packed the plates, cutlery and plastic glasses he'd spotted at the back of one of the cupboards into another bag, and then they all piled into the car.

"Where are we going, Daddy?" Adele asked as Martin buckled her into the back seat.

He kissed the tip of her cute nose and winked. "You'll find out soon enough. We're going on an adventure."

"Yay, I love adventures," Jake shouted eagerly.

Martin smiled at the lad. "I know you do, we've had a few over the past few months, haven't we?"

"I loved it when we went down the zip wires the best. Can we do that again soon, Martin?"

"Of course we can." He remembered the experience well; it had been a crucial moment in cementing their relationship.

"Daddy, why does he call you Martin?" Adele asked quietly.

"Because as much as I love Jake, I'm not his real daddy. I only have one child and that's you, honey. Do you understand?"

Her mouth twisted and her brow creased into a frown. "I think so. So Matilda and Jake aren't allowed to call you Daddy, like I am."

"That's right, sort of. They have a daddy of their own; it might get a little confusing for them if we start changing that, right, guys?" He looked across the seat at Matilda and Jake, who were both nodding.

Jake, who was sitting between the two girls, nudged Adele. "Hey, your dad is cool, much cooler than our dad. We rarely see our dad, do we, Mum?"

"No, love. That's unfortunate it has to be that way. But we're thankful Martin came into our lives, aren't we?"

Matilda and Jake both nodded. Adele turned to look at them. Martin observed her reaction. At first his daughter smiled at the other two children but, as though a with had flicked, the smile turned into a scowl. Matilda and Jake, who had been looking at Adele, suddenly turned to face ahead of them.

Martin was unsure whether to react or not. Instead, he decided to let the matter lie. He fastened his daughter's seatbelt and then ran around the other side of the car to check Jake and Matilda were both secured as well, before hopping into the driver's seat. He checked a postcode on his phone and entered it into the satnav.

"Are we ready for what awaits us, kids?"

"Yes, yes!" Jake and Matilda called back.

He looked in his mirror and saw Adele's eyes narrowed into small slits.

"Adele, honey, is there something wrong?"

A smile quickly slotted into place, and she looked him in the eye. "No, Daddy, everything is good, but thank you for asking."

Louise squeezed his thigh. "Hey, even I'm excited to see where you're taking us."

"Good. Enjoy the ride. It's not too far away, I promise, I wouldn't want you guys getting bored now, would I?"

"No chance of ever being bored with you around," Louise whispered and winked.

Martin smiled, his erection growing at the sight of her beautiful face. He shoved his selfish feelings aside, put the car into drive and set off. His hard-on thankfully subsided after a few minutes had passed.

"What if we play this CD on the way? It's got a few kids' stories on it. It'll help keep them occupied for a while," Louise suggested.

"And you didn't think to play it on the way up here, save us all from getting a sore throat due to our awful singing?"

"Sorry, in all honesty, I forgot about it until I found it lurking at the bottom of my bag this morning. My friend lent it to me."

"Crikey, and you actually found it in that bottomless pit you call a handbag?"

His quip earned him a jab in the thigh. "Cheeky. Yes or no?"

"Go for it. It'll give my voice a break anyway."

"Yeah, that was my idea behind the offer, too."

He faced her and shook his head. "Uncalled for retort, Louise, just saying."

She inserted the disc into the slot and David Walliams' voice filled the car. His soothing tone soon had the kids transfixed. Martin, grateful for Louise's intervention, drove to the secret location he'd sourced close by where they could spend the day. The road rose and dipped at regular intervals through the picturesque hills on either side. Thoughts of moving to the area flooded into his mind. He and Louise had been discussing a move away from Liverpool lately, but it had never gone further than that—a discussion. Maybe they could move here? Except, it was a two-and-a-half-hour drive back to Liverpool to visit Adele. *Maybe she could come and live with us, eventually?* Although, by the expression on her face right now, he couldn't see her wanting to do that anytime soon.

The signs for Wasdale Head started to appear at the side of the road. A thrill trickled through him. As soon as he and Louise had booked the cottage and asked Debs if Adele could join them for the week, Martin had sourced different possible places for them to visit. This place was high up on his list. The pictures on the internet didn't do it justice, though. The steep hills surrounding the lake appeared to take on a life of their own. He could imagine the setting in the gloomiest winter months and was glad they'd chosen to visit at the start of summer instead.

Matilda and Jake both gasped as they rounded the next bend and there, before them, in all its glory, was Wast Water. The peaks towering over the still lake were nothing short of breathtaking. He pulled into one of the lay-bys and admired the view himself for a few minutes.

"It's spectacular. How come I've never been here before?" Louise asked, mystified. "I don't think my parents ever discovered this place in all the times we visited the area."

"It drew my attention on the internet, I just had to come and check it out. Apparently, this is the deepest lake in England. Scaffel Pike, which is England's highest mountain, is just up the road. There's a hiking route from Wasdale Head up to the mountain. What do you think, kids, good choice of location?"

"Yes, can we go swimming?" Jake asked, straining in his seat to see the view over to Martin's right. Had his sister been sitting on that side of him instead of Adele, Martin felt Jake would have leaned over her, but he was a gent, through and through.

Their timing couldn't have been better either as at that moment the sun peeped out from behind a fluffy cloud, the sun's rays making it even more magical, illuminating the area. "Oh my, look at the awesome reflection of the hills on the water, it truly draws you in, doesn't it?" Louise said, her voice breathless from the wondrous display ahead of them.

"Let's see if we can park further up the road and get out, shall we?" It was a rhetorical question. Martin shifted the car into drive again and it crept forward. He couldn't help it, he kept one eye on the road and one eye on the scenery over to his right. Now and then, he glanced in the mirror to see the kids' faces all lit up in excitement and wonderment, even Adele's.

Louise pointed ahead. "What about there? There are a few cars parked in the spot already, but that shouldn't matter. I can't see anyone on the beach area."

"Maybe people park up and go for a trek around the lake. Wouldn't that be cool?"

Louise laughed. "One way of tiring the kids out, I suppose. Maybe we'll leave that for another day, eh?"

He pulled into a gap behind three other cars and they unloaded the bags from the boot. Martin grabbed a tartan blanket he always kept folded in there, and together, the five of them set off.

Louise insisted that Jake held his sister's hand while crossing the road, and Adele slotted into step between Louise and Martin. They picked their way down to the beach area that was a little stony. Just beyond that was the edge of the lake. The kids ran down and dipped their hands in.

"It's lovely and warm. Can we go in for a swim, Mum, please?" Jake's final word came out as a whining plea.

"Let's see if it warms up a little first," Louise shouted back. She glanced up at the sky overhead. "Are the clouds moving? I can't tell."

Martin shielded his eyes from the glare of the sun. "There are a few coming our way. Maybe hold fire for a while, Jake. See how the weather fares in half an hour or so and we'll reassess things then. Want to have a kick around instead?"

Jake's smile slipped and he kicked a stone into the water. "Okay, if I have to."

Great, another dissatisfied kid to deal with. Oh, well, here I go. "Can you watch Adele for me?"

Louise waved away the suggestion. "Goes without saying."

"We won't be able to play here, it's too stony. Why don't we go across the road to the fields over there? I don't think there are any sheep grazing, not from what I saw."

"Okay, just for half an hour and then can we come back and go for a swim?" Jake asked eagerly.

"We'll see. See you later, girls."

"Daddy, don't leave. I want to play with you, too," Adele's tone was broken and she seemed on the verge of tears.

Martin crouched in front of her and held her arms. "It's okay, sweetheart. We'll be over the road, just there. You stay with Louise for now, all right?"

Adele sniffled, her chin grazing her chest. "Okay," she murmured, sadly.

Louise motioned for him to leave Adele with her.

Martin smiled and kissed his daughter on the head. "I won't be long. I'll be back before you know it, I promise."

Adele slumped onto the pebbles and started throwing them, aiming at the water, but they fell short by quite a distance. Martin faced Louise and shrugged.

Louise mouthed for him to go and that she would watch over Adele.

Martin picked up the football and reached for Jake's hand to see him across the road and into the field opposite. They kicked the ball around and ended up over the far side of the grass. Before long, caught up in their game, Martin's competitive spirit came to the fore.

"Best of three in goal, all right?" he shouted to Jake.

"Bagsy shooting first."

"Go on, then." Martin and Jake both slipped off their jumpers and dropped them on the ground to act as goalposts. "Give it your best shot."

Jake took a run up and hit the ball powerfully. Martin threw himself to the right, but the ball squeezed underneath him. He grunted as he hit the ground.

"Yes, yes, one to me. I like this."

"It was a lucky shot. I'll be ready for you next time, squirt."

Martin rolled the ball back and danced on the line as Jake took a second run up to take another strike. This time, Jake sent Martin reeling to the left, but again, he failed to block the shot.

"Lucky, was I?" Jake shouted, laughing.

"Best of three, and remember, I've still got to shoot against you, buddy. Don't get too cocky now."

"Whatever. Are you ready, or do you need time to recover first?"

"Cheeky boy! Go on, make it your best shot yet, if you can."

Jake took another run up and then stopped; in the meantime, Martin had anticipated he was going to hit the ball to the right so pounced that way. Jake laughed and tapped the ball down the middle and then ran around, shouting, "I'm the winner," and waving his arms wildly.

Martin brushed himself down, slightly disgruntled. He fetched the ball that had reached the small hill behind him and peered over the top to see Adele, still sitting in the same position while Louise and Matilda were moving closer to the water's edge. Louise was calling out for Adele to join them, but his daughter only shook her head in response.

"Come on, slowcoach," Jake shouted, drawing his attention back to their game.

Martin lifted the ball, slotted it under one arm and spat into his palms. "That's it, I mean business now, Jake. You've awakened a wild animal within me and you're going to feel the full force of it now."

"Yeah, right." Jake rolled his eyes. "Bring it on!"

Jake took up his position between the two jumpers and jiggled about on the line. Martin eyeballed him, trying his hardest to psych him out, and then shot down the middle to score the first goal. "Yes, get in there, my beauty! Strike one!" He ran around in a small circle and punched the air.

Jake rolled the ball back out to him. "It's still three-one."

"We'll see about that!" Martin placed the ball down on the ground and eyed his opponent again. As soon as Jake made his move one way, he shot in the bottom corner in the opposite direction and bang, scored another goal. "Yes, and the maestro strikes again."

"No!" Jake stomped across the field and retrieved the ball. He kicked it back to Martin. "It's still three-two."

"Number three coming up, sonny."

They each took up their positions, one defensive and the other ready to let loose. Martin drew back his leg, but before he made contact with the ball, a crazed scream drew his attention.

It sounded like Louise.

He ran to the edge of the grass and looked across at where the girls were. Louise had Matilda standing in front of her. She saw him appear and yelled, "Martin, she's gone."

3

"What? Where's Adele?" His gaze darted around the area, searching for his daughter. She was nowhere to be seen. He called for Jake to join him, and together, they ran across the busy road.

Louise was beside herself, sobbing and shaking uncontrollably. "She's gone," she muttered again and again.

"How? When was the last time you saw her?"

"I don't know. I suppose four to five minutes ago. We have to find her. Oh, my God, what if she's in the water?"

"I told you to watch her," he shouted.

"Don't blame me. I was dealing with Matilda; she had a problem with her laces, I was teaching her how to tie them. When I looked up, Adele had gone. Maybe she went to find you. If you hadn't left her... she'd still be here."

He groaned and tugged at his hair. "Is that what it's come down to? The blame game? You told me you'd keep an eye on her while I was playing football with *your* son."

"*My* son and *your* daughter, is that what this is all about? I do my best, Martin, you should know that by now. Adele has made all this a struggle. She barely talks."

Martin held up a warning finger and shook his head. "Don't even go there. Not now. I have to find her." He began a desperate search of the area and turned back to Louise. "Don't just stand there, make yourself useful and ring the damn police. They need to come, tell them it's urgent."

He raced to the water's edge along the small beach area they'd chosen, but couldn't see anything there. So he bolted in the opposite direction towards the road and checked up and down it to see if Adele had wandered off that way. Again, nothing.

Frantically, he searched behind every visible mound he could see within spitting distance of where he'd left his daughter. Each time he found nothing, his heart sank a little deeper. His eyes misted over with unshed tears. *Stay strong. She's out here somewhere, I just need to find her!*

It took twenty minutes of nerve-wracking searching, getting further and further away from where he'd left his daughter to play a damn game of football, before the police eventually showed up. He heard the siren and ran back to where he'd left Louise and her two kids.

One measly patrol car, was that all his daughter was worth to these people? Two uniformed officers were speaking to Louise. She was gripping both her children tightly in front of her. Jealousy surged within him. *Why couldn't she have held Adele close like that? Why didn't I?* His thoughts were all over the place, as well as his emotions. Anger and fear being the most prominent. He was angry with all of them, including himself.

"Here's Martin now," Louise said as he got closer to the two officers, one female and the other male, both young, just starting out by the look of things.

I don't need the likes of them, I need experienced officers on this damn case. I want my daughter back.

"Hello, sir. PCs Carter and Millward at your assistance," the male officer said, a blank expression settled on his face.

"Is this it? Is this all you're prepared to do out in this neck of the woods when kids go missing?"

"Initially, yes, sir. It's our duty to report our findings before other departments get involved."

His blood seared through his veins. "Are you kidding me? My daughter is fucking out there, missing, and all you're prepared to do is send two novice police officers to attend." He turned on the spot and ran a hand through his hair. "What the actual fuck!"

"Martin, you need to calm down and stop swearing at the officers, it's not helping anyone," Louise warned.

He faced her, his eyes narrowed as he assessed the way she was clinging on to her own children. Anger bubbling up inside, he shouted, "How dare you stand there and tell me to calm down while gripping your own children that way? How bloody dare you!"

Louise appeared stung by his brutal words. Matilda and Jake clung to their mother and began sobbing.

Great, you bastard, see what you've done now. "I'm sorry. I was wrong to say that, Louise." He faced the officers again. "Please, you need to get a search party out here. She's here somewhere, I'm going out of my mind knowing that she could be getting further and further away from us while we stand around here doing fuck all." His irritation mounted as Adele's scared face entered his mind. He balled his fists to prevent his hands from shaking.

"We need to take a statement from you both first. The quicker we do that, the sooner we can get the search underway."

Martin glared at the male copper, seething, but wisely refrained from kicking off again. "Here's my statement: I was over on the other side of the road playing football with Jake. I left my daughter here, sitting right here, with Louise looking after her." He glanced at his girl-friend and saw the tears slip onto her cheeks. "Jesus, you think crying is going to help us?"

The male officer, Carter, leaned over and whispered something in his partner's ear. She reacted instantly by walking towards Louise and the kids and steering them away from Martin and the male officer.

"Sir, I'm going to need you to remain calm. Having a pop at people who are trying to help you isn't going to get you very far."

"You reckon? Jesus, all I want is my five-year-old daughter back. If she's out there, lost, she's going to be petrified out of her mind. I'm not going to apologise for being a concerned father. How would you feel if this was your daughter?"

"I can't begin to imagine, sir. I have a three-year-old at home and my wife and I never let her out of our sight."

Martin's head jutted forward. "Shit! Did you seriously just say that? Fuck, I was keeping someone else's kid occupied while that someone was supposed to be watching out for my child. She screwed up, not me. Had I not been putting someone else's child first, then my daughter would still be here, safe and unharmed with me. Am I making myself clear here? I'm not at fault."

"Does it really matter who is at fault, sir? It's not helping anyone by blaming others, is it?"

"It's making me feel a whole lot better, I can tell you." He rubbed his neck and sighed, frustration coming to the fore. "No... actually, it's frigging not. My head is in a bloody spin. Please, you have to help us. She's out there somewhere. Isn't there a mountain rescue team around here? I thought I read there was."

"Yes, there is. I need to report back with my findings before we can action getting them involved."

"What are you waiting for, then? I can't tell you anything else, it's Louise you need to speak to; she was supposed to be watching over my daughter."

"I gathered that much, sir. I'll have a word with her. Maybe you could watch the kids for her, would that be possible?"

His gaze drifted towards Louise, but she had her back turned to him and rage erupted inside. "No, I can't do that, not after the way she's failed me." An unimaginable pain clutched his chest. "Help me get my child back, please!"

"I'll get my colleague to watch over the kids. I understand how fragile the situation is, sir."

"Fragile? That's one word for it, I suppose. Just get on with it. It'll be dark soon at this rate." Martin knew he was talking out of his arse—it was barely eleven o'clock, but his urgency to find his daughter knew no bounds.

Carter walked away and joined Louise, her two children and the female officer. He spoke quietly to the two women. Louise glanced his way and shook her head, her expression crushed. She urged her children to stay with the female officer and took a few paces to the right to speak to Carter. Martin observed the pair of them whilst still trying to survey the surrounding area, just in case Adele came back.

Louise glanced his way periodically during the time she was giving her account of the events. He didn't have it in him to smile or show any kind of warmth towards the woman he'd fallen in love with over the past few months.

How can I forgive her stupidity? Why should I? Her kids are fine, neither of them has gone missing.

No, it's my beautiful Adele.

Honey, be safe. Come back if you've wandered off, come back to me. I need you. I won't be able to go on with my life knowing that you've gone.

After around ten minutes, Carter returned.

"Well, what did she say?" Martin demanded.

"That her daughter tripped over her shoelaces and had twisted her ankle. She was caring for Matilda, showing her how to tie her laces properly when she happened to glance up, and that's when she noticed Adele was missing. She's not at fault, sir, no one is. These things happen. Adele will be found; kids have a habit of wandering off, to explore the intriguing landscape around them."

"Bullshit. Just file your report and get the others up here to help. I can't do this on my own. You need to help me."

"I'll do that now. I want to assure you, you're not alone, sir."

Martin bit down the sarcastic retort scorching his tongue. He looked over at the road where a crowd had gathered. He was tempted to go over there and shout at them for being insensitive, gawping like that, but thought better of it. Instead, he tugged on Carter's sleeve while he was requesting backup on his radio.

"Hang on," he said to the person on control. "What is it, sir, have you seen something?"

"You need to ask them," he said, pointing at the rubberneckers, "see if any of them saw anything."

Carter peered over his shoulder. "All in good time, sir. Let me summon more officers and then I'll ask the crowd."

"Okay, my bad. Sorry." He paced the area, agitated by the officer's reprimand, until he finished talking into the radio. "Now will you go and see what they have to say?"

"In a moment. Just to bring you up to date on how things stand, more officers are on the way and the mountain rescue team has been dispatched. This place will be inundated with the emergency services in no time at all."

"Excellent, it's what I would expect if a child went missing," he snapped, itching to swipe the smug grin off the young officer's face.

Carter took the hint and set off to speak to the crowd which had grown considerably in the few minutes he'd been on the radio.

Martin spent the next five minutes sizing up each of the onlookers, observing their mannerisms. Most of the women appeared horrified, as did some of the men. There was a lot of head shaking going on, which made him despondent.

It was another thirty minutes before additional officers showed up. Two patrol cars and an unmarked car arrived, followed by a Land Rover with several people on board. Organised chaos ensued for the next few minutes until a plan had been formed by the rescue team. Carter apprised the newcomers of the situation. The head of the rescue team approached Martin. "We're going to do our very best to find your daughter, sir. Can I ask if you have anything belonging to your daughter to hand? It's so our dogs can follow her scent."

"No, oh God, I don't think I have anything with me. Louise," he called out, "Can you think of anything Adele touched so they can pick up her scent?"

Louise thought it over for a second but shook her head. "Only back at the cottage."

"Great, that's at least thirty minutes away from here."

The volunteer rescuer smiled. "Don't worry, we'll do the best we can. If we struggle to find her, I might have to ask you to return to the cottage and fetch something for us, if that's okay?"

"Yes, just say the word. Please, do your best. She's only five, she'll be scared shitless out there on her own."

"Does she have any medical problems we should know about?"

"No, I don't think so. No, I'm certain she doesn't. Shit! Should I ring her mother to find out? We're separated. Damn, if I tell her she's missing, she's going to come down on me like a bloody ton of bricks. I can't ring her yet, not now. I'm going to leave it a while, just in case we find her. Sorry, I'm rambling."

"It's fine, don't worry. We'll set off now. Hopefully, we'll have good news for you soon."

As he walked away, a young woman wearing a navy-blue suit approached him with a man of similar age by her side. She produced a warrant card.

"Hello, Mr Jenkins, I'm DI Samantha Cobbs and this is my partner DS Bob Jones. I'm sorry to hear about your daughter. Would you mind going over what happened?"

Martin groaned. "Do I have to keep repeating myself? Can't you get all the facts from Carter? All I want to do is find my daughter and all you lot seem intent on doing is wasting frigging time."

"I understand your frustration, sir, if you'll bear with us for a few minutes more. Can you tell me how long your daughter has been missing now?"

"No, I can't. Because I haven't been clock-watching. Jesus, take my word for it, will you? She's missing. She's five years old, do you realise what that means? She's out there, all alone. Probably panicking, terrified that she won't be found. God help me, do something, please."

"We will, Mr Jenkins. We have people scouring the area, you know that. It's our job to search for the reasons why your child might have walked off."

He frowned and asked, "What are you insinuating? I have to say, I don't like the tone of voice you're using."

"I didn't mean it to come across badly. What I'm asking is if you perhaps shouted at her. Could she have gone off in a huff, you know, like kids do?"

He tutted. "I repeat, she's five. As far as I know, kids that age don't tend to wander off in unknown territory."

"I appreciate that. So what do you suggest has happened to her, then?"

He closed his eyes and shook his head. "Bloody hell, if I knew that do you really think I'd be standing around here talking to you idiots?"

"Name-calling isn't going to help, sir. We're doing our best with the limited facts you've given us so far."

Inhaling and exhaling to calm his shattered nerves, Martin said, "Then it's not me you should be speaking to, it's Louise; she was in charge of my daughter at the time she went missing."

"And who is Louise to you, your wife?"

"Hardly. No, my girlfriend. Who knows how long that is going to last, unless you find my daughter?"

"I see. Has the relationship been fraught for a while, then?" Cobbs asked while Jones jotted down the details in his little black book.

"No. This was a family holiday. Adele's mother and I are separated, she lives with her. I've spent the past eight months battling the court system, trying to get access to my daughter and now... well, this has fucking happened. Deborah is going to crucify me." He covered his face with his hands and forced back the tears threatening to emerge.

"I'm sorry, that must have been a stressful time for you."

He dropped his hands and nodded. "It was. This holiday was about getting to know my daughter all over again and now... she's gone. Please, you have to find her. To bring her back to me. I'm distraught. I know I'm coming across as a hard bastard, but it's only because I care. She means the world to me, please help me find her."

"We're going to do what we can to help you. Have you informed her mother?"

"No, I don't want to do that, not yet. Can't we leave it for another couple of hours? What harm will it do? Maybe we'll find her in that time."

"Keeping another parent in the dark isn't something I would

33

recommend, sir. It's your call, for now. If it were down to me, I would inform the mother right away. If the boot was on the other foot, you would want to know, wouldn't you?"

He stared at the pebbles beneath his feet and dragged his foot over a larger one. "I suppose you're right. She's going to be furious. Even if Adele comes back to us, I doubt whether Debs will ever let me see her again after this debacle."

"You might be doing your ex-partner an injustice there. Either way, she has a right to know. Why don't I ring her now?"

Defeated, Martin reached for his mobile that he kept in his rear pocket. He scrolled through his contacts and handed his phone to the sergeant. After jotting the number down, the sergeant thanked him.

DI Cobbs punched the number into her phone and placed the call. Martin listened to her side of the conversation, knowing damn well how Debs was going to react on the other end. Suddenly, the inspector passed her phone over to Martin. "She wants to speak with you."

He closed his eyes for a split second and gulped, then took the phone from the inspector. "Hello, Deborah."

"Martin, what the *fuck* is going on? Where the hell is my daughter?"

"I'm sorry. I can't tell you that. *Our* daughter is missing, and I don't have a clue either what likely happened to her or where she might be."

Deborah screamed and then began to sob. His hard heart softened a touch.

"How is that possible when she was in your care?" she finally demanded through her tears.

"I was playing football with Jake and took my eye off her for a second and when I looked back, she was gone." The inspector tilted her head at the lie. He shrugged and covered the phone. "I can't tell her the truth."

"You should. She deserves to know the truth," the inspector whispered back.

He shook his head and kept up the pretence. "She must have wandered off, Debs. We have the emergency services here, the rescue team has just set off. I didn't want to pester you with this; it was the inspector's decision to get you involved, not mine."

"What? You're telling me that if the inspector hadn't forced your hand, I would be none the wiser about our child's disappearance? Is that what it's come to? You really hate me that much, Martin? I know the court has made your life hell recently, but that wasn't down to me. It was the system's fault you haven't had any contact with Adele, not mine."

"I don't believe you. If you'd only had the decency to back off, none of this would have happened. My daughter no longer knows me, she's been like a stranger around us since I bloody picked her up."

"What the fuck?" Debs sucked in a sharp intake of breath and then let rip. "How can you tell me that and then inform me you left her to her own devices while you took care of another woman's child, placing their needs before your own flesh and blood? You selfish fucking bastard."

Martin held the phone away from his ear. Hearing the truth drove another stake through his heart. "This is why I didn't want to tell her," he sneered at the inspector.

The inspector shrugged. "The child's legal guardian has a right to know, you should know that."

"I would have told her in my own time," he informed the inspector before replacing the phone to his ear to hear Debs' further tirade of abuse.

"You have never treated our daughter right. You don't deserve to have the title of father as you've never been there for her, not after you ran out on me."

"And whose fault was that?"

Debs gasped. "Why, you, downright piece of scum."

"This isn't helping, Deborah. For your information, I feel like shit, but rant away—selfish as usual, discounting anyone else's feelings in the process."

"Screw you. No, don't, I've already done that and it wasn't a pleasurable experience. The only good thing that came out of our time together was Adele, and now, you've fucking *lost* her."

"Don't hold back, say what you mean, Debs. You can't make me feel any worse than I do right now, I can assure you. I'm handing you back to the inspector, thanks for your support and understanding, as usual."

Before she could fire off another bout of abuse, he shoved the phone back in the inspector's hand.

"Hello, Deborah, it's DI Cobbs again. Yes… I assure you, we won't let you down. The team is here in force. If your daughter is out there, we will find her. You need to have faith in us… yes, okay, I'll pass that message on to Martin. Take care, hopefully we'll be in touch with some good news for you soon." The inspector ended the call and tucked her mobile into her jacket pocket. "She asked me to pass on her apologies for having a go at you. I'm sure you'll forgive her in the circumstances; you're both fraught, and emotions are running high, off the scale probably."

"Well, at least that's one thing. You have to understand, Inspector, none of this was deliberate. We're just a family on holiday, trying to ensure the kids have fun. The fact we took our eye off Adele for a moment will haunt us until she comes back to us. Please, please make that happen." His gaze drifted to the lake, and he pointed at the inviting still water that always seemed to mesmerise younger children. "Shouldn't you be searching the lake?"

"In time. That will be our last resort. There's every possibility she could be close by, hiding behind a craggy rock or any of the numerous mounds of grass in the nearby fields."

"Okay, I hear you. What do you need me to do? I can't stand around here doing nothing, it wouldn't be right."

"Maybe set off in that direction, don't go too far. Call out her name. She'll be scared, hearing your familiar voice might encourage her to come out of her hiding place. Keep it light and simple. Don't let her pick up on your frustration or anger, it could have a detrimental effect."

"Grant me with some sense." He stormed off towards the road and muttered, "Fucking coppers know fuck all about how to deal with kids." *Hmm… maybe that could be aimed at me, too. Otherwise, my darling Adele would be with us now.*

Louise called out to him, "Martin, come back. Where are you going?"

"To search for my daughter. You know, the one you took your eye off."

He switched off, ignoring Louise's wounded response. He was hurting too, inside and out. All he wanted was to hold Adele, to comfort her and tell her everything was going to be all right. He struggled to fight the sensation that he would never see his daughter again, not until he passed away and met up with her in heaven.

Shit! I can't think that way. I'll find her, if it takes every last breath in my body to do it.

4

$\mathcal{M}$artin searched the immediate area high and low for over an hour, keeping a constant eye on what the emergency services were doing around him at the same time.

Louise, Matilda and Jake had drifted back to the car. He felt no remorse for speaking to Louise the way he had; he couldn't get past the truth—all this was her fault. He needed someone else to blame other than himself. Deborah was correct to point out the obvious. He shouldn't have been off playing with Jake; he should have sat down with Adele, seen to her needs, tried to get reacquainted with her after the months they'd spent apart. *All well and good thinking that when it's too late.*

He wandered back to where the inspector and sergeant were standing. The inspector was issuing orders to the latest arrivals: another six uniformed coppers, a mixture of genders. When the group dispersed to carry out their instructions, Martin drifted closer. "Can I have a word?"

"A quick one. What do you need to know, Mr Jenkins?"

"It's Martin." The inspector nodded. "Where are we at?"

"As you can see, more and more officers have come to join in the search. I've asked a couple of them to begin taking down the witness statements. After speaking with the crowd, I have to tell you, it's not good news. No one saw or heard anything out of the ordinary, not until Louise cried out."

"Helpful... not!"

"It is what it is. Hopefully, the rescue team will report back with their findings soon. Maybe you can search the car for anything that belongs to Adele; I know you said the likelihood was negligible, but it might be worth a try."

He looked back at the car. Louise was staring at him, her mouth down at the sides. She wiped her nose on a tissue and then twisted in her seat to speak to Matilda and Jake. He was undecided whether to approach the car or not after treating her so badly.

How could he take the damaging words back, even if he wanted to?

The truth was, she'd let him down. As much as he didn't want to dwell on it, how could he bear to look at her in the same way ever again? This was an incomprehensible mistake to make by anyone's standards. How did one even begin trying to defend Louise's actions? *On the other hand, why should I? If Adele had gone missing while I was watching her, people would be whipping my arse good and proper for letting my daughter down.*

"Go on, you're going to have to speak to each other sooner or later," the inspector urged, appearing to read his mind.

He faced her and shook his head. "I can't, not yet, it's too painful. I know this was a simple accident, but the fact remains the same: she should have been keeping a vigilant eye on Adele, that lapse in responsibility is hard to accept."

The inspector sighed and shook her head. "You're being too hard on her. If you didn't trust her, why leave your child with her in the first place?"

"You've twisted my words, I never said I didn't trust her. Never mind, I need to be alone for a while, to wallow in self-pity, if you will. The last thing I want to do right now is go over there and tell Louise everything is going to be all right and that I forgive her, because I haven't got it in me to do that. Not yet... maybe I'll never be able to do it. Perhaps I should send her and her little family packing; I'll stay here alone to try and find Adele. Yes, that's what I'll do."

He went to walk back to the car, but the inspector grabbed his arm. "You'd be wise to mull that thought over a few times before you decide to put it into action. I fear if you take that route, there'll be no going back in the future. Is that what you truly want? To mess up your support network?"

He shrugged her arm off and expelled a large breath. "I'm confused, I don't know what I want. No, I do, I want my daughter back in my arms, but I can't see that happening anytime soon, can you? You might be thinking I'm a right bastard for acting this way, but answer me this... how the hell would you be reacting if it was your child who had gone missing? Do you think you'd be skipping around here, whooping with joy? I doubt it." Annoyed, he ran a hand around the back of his neck. "Anyway, don't tell me you're not trying to weigh up my reactions, in the hope I might slip up and reveal that I'm behind my daughter's disappearance after all."

Inspector Cobbs raised an eyebrow, glanced at the lake as if biting back a snarky response, then her attention was drawn back to him. "If you think that, Martin, then I have to tell you that you're gravely mistaken. I believe you, I believe *in* you, and Louise come to that. This was a genuine mistake and apportioning the blame isn't going to get you, as a family, anywhere. Go over there and make your peace with Louise, for all your sakes. While you're there, see if there is anything in the car belonging to Adele that the rescue dogs can use for tracking."

"Okay, I'll go and do that. As for speaking to Louise... well, I'm sorry, I don't think I'd be able to keep my anger in check long enough to hold a conversation with her."

"That's your prerogative. I'm putting it on record that you're wrong in your decision-making."

He grunted and trudged over to the car on weary, heavy legs. The fight in him was dwindling fast and he sensed exhaustion was about to hit him with a devastating force.

Louise smiled as he opened the car door. "How's it going?" she asked, her voice hoarse with emotion.

"It's going. I'm not here to chat. I've come to search the car for any of Adele's possessions, to give to the rescue team. Apparently, the dogs will be able to pick up on the scent."

"Good thinking. Matilda, Jake, is there anything in the back that belongs to Adele? Look on the floor, under the seats, if you will."

"Here, I've found this." Jake held up a small fluffy cow with a keyring attached. "She was playing with it for a while on the way up here."

Martin smiled at Jake. "Thanks, you're a star, Jake. I'll get this back to them."

Louise reached for his hand. He snatched it away before she could touch his flesh. "Martin, don't push me away. I feel bad enough as it is. Please, don't punish me further."

"I'm not. Maybe that's your guilty conscience pricking you." He slammed the door shut and ran back to the inspector. "We found this. Jake said Adele was playing with it on the way here yesterday. Will it do?"

The inspector took a latex glove out of her pocket and snapped it on. "The less added scents on it, the better, I think. It'll help, I'm sure it will."

"Sorry, I should have thought about that."

"It's fine, I wouldn't expect you to consider it as evidence." She looked behind her. "There's a member of the team now. I'll give it to her."

He watched the inspector trot over to the Land Rover and hand the keyring to the female rescuer, who accepted it with a nod and a smile. Then the inspector returned to tell him, "She thinks it'll make a huge difference. She's put in a call to summon the dog handlers back from the search."

Martin held up his crossed fingers. "Thank God. I hope it helps." His gaze drifted skywards at the darkening clouds overhead. "Looks like it's going to piss down soon."

"I just said the same to my people. I'm sure it won't hamper the search. Have faith that we will find her. How did things go with Louise?"

He shook his head and sighed. "Not good. I backed away as soon as Jake handed me the keyring. I haven't got room in my heart to forgive and forget just yet."

"I suppose it will take time."

*F*our hours later, Martin was sitting on the grassy bank, wet through after yet another storm cloud had unburdened its heavy load over the picturesque area.

"Martin, you need to get out of those wet clothes," Louise said, just behind him.

"I know what I need to do, and it's not that. Go back to the car."

"How long are we expected to wait here? The kids are getting anxious and restless."

"*Your* kids, you mean. My child is still missing, in case you hadn't noticed."

"Can you change the record, Martin? I'm done with your accusatory tone. For the last time, I'm sorry. Why can't you accept my apology and move on?"

He pushed up onto his feet and stood nose to nose with her. Louise shrunk back as if she feared he was about to strike her. "Don't push me, Louise. You have no idea of the turmoil going on in my head or in my heart. My child, my five-year-old daughter, is out there on her own. Probably shit-scared and hurt for all we know, and you're standing there telling me that your damn kids are getting restless. Jesus, have a heart, woman. Put someone else's concerns before your own for a change."

Louise turned to walk away, her shoulders rising and falling as the tears emerged. "You're a heartless bastard. I'll get a lift back to the cottage, pack up our stuff and head back to Liverpool. I'm done with you treating me like a piece of shit, like a fucking stranger."

"Don't bother getting a lift. Here, take my keys." He threw the car keys, and they landed in a puddle by her feet.

She swivelled to face him. "What? How will you get home?"

"Who cares? I'll stay here until my daughter is found. I refuse to stop searching for her. Others might, but I won't."

Just then, a car screeched to a halt alongside them, drawing Martin's attention away from Louise.

"Oh, great, that's all I effing need," he grumbled as he watched Debs exit the vehicle and tear across the muddy bank towards them.

She stood in front of him and demanded, "Any news?"

"No. Not yet. What in God's name are you doing here? You should have left all this to me. I was going to keep in touch with you. There was no need for you to drive all this way."

"I had to come. You would have done the same, if you were in my position. I could no longer sit staring at the phone, willing it to ring. She's my daughter; I have a right to know what's going on when it happens, not second-hand with details omitted by my angry ex."

"As if I would? Jesus, grant me some sense, Deborah. Get back in the car and go to a hotel or something. I could do without the extra stress of having you around here."

"I refuse to. Who's in charge? Where's that inspector I spoke with earlier?"

He pointed at the police car on the other side of the road. "She's in there, keeping warm with her sidekick, I shouldn't wonder."

"That's not fair, Martin. You know as well as I do, she's only just got back in the car after hours of standing around out in the rain," Louise piped up.

"Whatever. If I'm out here in the wet, then she should be as well. Anyway, what are you still doing here? I told you to go home."

Debs' gaze flitted between them. "What's going on here? Why are you angry with Louise?"

He shrugged, held his arms out to the side and let them drop again. "I didn't tell you over the phone. It was Louise who was watching over Adele when she went missing."

Louise's head dipped and she mumbled an apology.

Debs instantly flew at Louise, fists and nails striking her body and face. Louise just stood there and accepted her punishment. In the end, it was Martin who intervened, pulling Debs away from his girlfriend who was now cowering from the attack.

Jake ran across and flung his arms around his mother's waist. "Leave my mummy alone," he shouted.

Debs sobbed and hid her face. "I'm so sorry. Sorry. Sorry, I didn't mean to attack you."

Louise glared at Martin and Debs, then flung her arms around her son. "Come on, Jake, let's go home."

That was the last interaction Martin had with her that day. His heart sank deeper than it ever had before. He tentatively placed an arm around Debs' shoulders. "It's okay. She'll be fine. Come on, let's get you in the car." He guided her back to her vehicle and saw Inspector Cobbs coming their way.

"What was that all about?" the inspector demanded to know.

"A misunderstanding. You wanted me to tell Debs the truth; you witnessed the outcome of that deed."

"Jesus, is Louise all right?"

"I suggest you ask her that question, not me," Martin said. He peered over his shoulder and heard Louise start the car. "You'd better be quick, she's on her way back to Liverpool."

"What? Without you?"

"Yes. I can't stand to be around her and her kids a moment longer. And yes, I feel like a bastard for saying that, but it happens to be the truth."

"You have a bizarre way of dealing with this situation, Mr Jenkins. I fear you're going to regret your actions in the days to come, months even."

"Maybe I will. At the moment, it feels like the right thing to do. Now, if you don't mind, Debs needs to hear all the facts from me."

"I can't disagree with that. Nice to meet you, Deborah. I want to assure you, the team are still out there doing their best to find Adele."

"Good. How long is the search going to last? These things have a time limit I take it?" Debs asked.

"Any case I work will be in accordance with the guidelines set out by headquarters. It depends if any clues or evidence surfaces."

"Has there been any so far?" Debs swiped at a tear which had slipped onto her cheek.

"No. Sadly, nothing has come to light as yet. We're hopeful something will show up soon."

"Before the night descends, you forgot to add that part, Inspector."

Martin nodded. "Yes, what happens then?"

"Hopefully, it won't come to that. I've called for extra backup, volunteers are joining in the hunt. I'm sure it's only a matter of time before she's found. Please, keep faith in us and what we're doing."

"It's hard, especially when you've all been at it for hours and are no further forward, Inspector," Martin reminded her unnecessarily. "Come on, get back in the car, Debs."

"I'll leave you to it. Will you be sticking around?" Cobbs asked.

"Of course. We'll sleep in the car if we have to. I'm sure Debs will agree with me."

"Yes, I agree. We need to be here in case Adele finds her way back. One thing that rattled through my mind on the journey up here…"

The inspector inclined her head and asked. "What's that, Deborah?"

"Are you looking into the possibility that Adele was taken? Abducted?"

"No, don't say that!" Martin pleaded. He released his hold on Debs and paced back and forth. "Why haven't we considered that?"

"It's something that has crossed our minds, Martin. We've asked all the witnesses if they saw anyone walking with a child, but none of them had, so I put the thought to bed. It's a tough call to make. I suggest, in the interim, we stick to the idea that Adele has wandered off."

He frowned. "Really? Why would you dismiss the other theory so easily?"

"I haven't. I've already stated we questioned the witnesses who were in the area at the time and drew a blank. We'll keep both options open, if you'd prefer it that way."

"Yes, we would. What about a media splash, aren't you going to bother with one of those?"

"I was in the process of doing just that when Deborah arrived. I witnessed the fracas between the three of you and jumped out of the car to intervene."

"And? How did you get on?"

"These things take time to arrange, Martin. I can't flick my fingers and summon the relative parties to be here, just like that."

"Unfortunately, I fear time is a commodity we are running out of, don't you?"

Cobbs nodded. "Possibly, which is why I've summoned more troops and asked for the police helicopter to be dispatched."

"What? Why wasn't that done immediately?"

"Because, in our experience, when a child wanders off, they invariably return within a few hours. It would have been a waste of time and resources bringing the chopper in sooner."

Martin's rage mounted. "Are you for real? Do you realise how bloody serious this situation is?"

"I would advise you to keep calm, Martin. Try not to say anything that you may later regret."

He took a few paces towards her, and Debs pulled on his arm to prevent him from doing anything foolish. "Oh, that would be your expert advice, would it? Why don't you share with us what you intend to do if our child isn't found by the time it gets dark?"

The inspector stood her ground and held eye contact with him. "We're doing our best, sir. If you feel it's not good enough, then you can always raise a complaint. I can give you the information you need to do that, if you require it."

"Martin, this isn't helping. Please, don't ruin this for Adele. Think what the consequences could be if you ask someone else to take over at this late stage. I'm sure the inspector is doing her best for us."

"Thank you, Deborah. I can assure you, I'm ensuring everyone is doing what is necessary to find your child."

Taking a step back, Martin sighed. "I'm sorry. Blame it on the situation. I'm not usually this angry. Tell her, Debs. After all that we've been through in the last few months, the trauma of not seeing my daughter because of the damned court's interference, I've never once showed the frustration and anger eating me up inside, have I?"

"It's true. He's done his very best to keep his emotions in check throughout such a tense situation. Please forgive his outburst and continue what you're doing for us."

"I will. You have my word. Believe me, I totally understand all the emotional baggage you're having to contend with right now."

"Okay, you'll have to forgive my outbursts at times, it's just my frustration talking."

The inspector gave a curt nod. "I'm prepared to do that. Please, I'm concerned that you've been out in this weather for hours now, you'll be no use to anyone if you catch pneumonia. Why don't you both sit in the car? I'll report back to you if any news comes through on the radio, I promise."

Debs hooked her arm through his. "She's right. Come on, let's get in my car. Wait, Inspector, is there anywhere around here where we can get a hot drink and something to eat, perhaps?"

"Yes, there are a couple of hotels up the road. Let me get something organised for you, rather than you leave the area. Will a sandwich do for now?"

"Martin?"

"Yes, okay, I'm not fussed. I probably won't eat it, but a white coffee with two sugars would be good. Thanks."

"Deborah, what about you?"

"White coffee with one sugar will do and a tuna sandwich on brown, if you don't mind. I'll get you some money, it's in the car."

"Nonsense, I've got this. I'll be back soon."

They watched the inspector walk away. "She's doing her best for us, Martin, go easy on her, eh?"

He turned to Debs and smiled weakly. "I never thought I'd hear myself say this again after everything we've been through, but I'm glad you're here with me."

She reached up and touched his face. "Where else would I be? She's our life, isn't she? Come on, let's sit in the car, it's getting colder and wetter by the minute."

He stood there, staring at the landscape beyond. "Yes, and she's out there, somewhere, scared shitless, probably thinking we've abandoned her."

Debs sniffled and wiped her nose on the sleeve of her coat. "We mustn't think that. She knows how much we love her. Keep the faith that she'll come back to us soon."

They trudged back to Debs' car and she started the engine and flicked on the heater to help dry them out. They both remained silent for the next few minutes, appraising the activity going on all around them.

Ten minutes or so later, a uniformed officer knocked on the passenger window; he had two cups and a bag in his hand. Martin lowered the window and accepted the goodies. "Thanks. Will you pass on our gratitude to the inspector?"

"I will, sir. Enjoy." The young male officer nodded and rejoined the rest of his team.

Martin passed the bag and the coffee with the number one marked on the top to Debs. "I think this must be yours."

"Thanks, do you want to try half a sandwich? Go on, you should eat something, if only to keep your strength up for what lies ahead of us. That's the only reason I'm eating, there's no telling if I'll be able to swallow anything past the huge lump in my throat."

"I'm sorry I messed up," he murmured, taking a sip from his coffee.

"You didn't. If it was a genuine mistake, then no one is to blame. I feel shit after the way I attacked Louise."

"She deserved it."

Debs turned in her seat to face him. "Is everything all right between you two?"

"Hardly. I told her to pack her bags, take the car and go home. I can't bear to look at her right now, knowing she was responsible." He bit down on his tongue. Should he be revealing what was going on in his personal life to her, of all people, his ex?

"You're wrong to believe that, Martin. She'll be as torn up about Adele as we are. More so, if she was supposed to be looking after our little girl."

"I can't forgive her for putting her own child before ours."

Debs took a bite of her sandwich and offered him the other half, still in the paper bag. "Take it, it's scrummy. If her child was in trouble, then she did the right thing tending to her; you and I would have done the same in her shoes."

"Are you sure about that?" He tore the bag open and took a bite of the sandwich. He was hungrier than he thought in spite of the deep foreboding feeling ripping at his insides.

"No, I'm not sure. I'm trying to act as peacemaker here. Louise doesn't deserve to be treated like a leper. She'll be as cut up about this as we are, even worse now that you've rejected her."

He set the bag aside, dug into his jeans pocket and pulled out a small box. He opened it, and inside was a sapphire and diamond engagement ring. "I was going to propose to her today, in this beautiful setting, with the children all around us."

Debs gasped. "Damn. That's such a shame. Beautiful ring, by the way. Put it aside, I'm sure once Adele comes back to us, you two will be fine again."

He shook his head. "I doubt it. I can't believe how well you're taking it. I thought you'd be hysterical."

"Maybe you don't know me as well as you think you do. Now I'm here, I can see how hard people are working to find our baby. If I'd stayed in Liverpool, there's no way I would've been able to hold things together." She reached for his hand, and he put his sandwich down and slipped his hand into hers. "We'll get through this together, honey. Put all the angst we've been through lately aside and concentrate on thinking positively about getting our baby back. Our baby needs us to be strong. Together, we can be as strong as we need to be; separately, we'll both be floundering around like lost souls."

He looked at her, and a slight smile tugged at his lips. "Deep down, you're a good woman, Debs. Remind me, why did we split up again?"

She laughed. "Oh gosh, we really don't want to revisit all that again. Let's live for today and put the past behind us, for our daughter's sake. Eat up, our food is getting cold."

He chuckled and studied his sandwich. "Idiot. Thank you, for being you and for coming all this way to be with me."

"Well, I didn't just jump in the car and drive up here to be with you, but if it'll help put you in a better mood to think that, then who am I to stop you?" She bit into her sandwich and groaned. "Much better than stopping off to buy a Greggs' sandwich."

"Yuck, the thought of it. There's no comparison." He continued to tuck into his half until his eye caught something going on ahead of him. "I wonder what's going on. I need to find out." He put his cup and the remains of his sandwich in the footwell and shot out of the car before Debs could stop him.

He raced towards the inspector who was chatting to one of the mountain rescue team dog handlers. "What's up? Have you found something?" he pleaded.

Debs came up behind him and placed an arm around his waist. Instinctively, he flung an arm around her shoulder and pulled her close. "Have you found her?" she asked, her voice filled with hope.

The rescuer, who was in his late thirties and sporting a goatee beard, gave them a weary smile. "I'm sorry, not yet. The dog picked up on her scent, but then lost it."

"How do you know that?" Martin asked, confused.

"Using the keyring you gave us, she followed the scent to the edge of the road and then stared up at me; from experience, I know that the trail has gone cold for her."

"So you gave up? Is that what you're telling me?" Martin demanded.

"Martin, please, that's not what Jeff said at all," Inspector Cobbs jumped in.

"Oh right, my mistake." He flung an arm in the air. "What are you doing about it, then?"

"We continued to search the area, but she kept returning to the spot."

"Thank you, Jeff. Will you keep trying for us?" Cobbs asked.

"Of course, but I'm telling you now, there's no point once the trail has been lost."

"What about the rain? Does that have a bearing on the scent?" the inspector asked.

"Not really, it can affect it slightly, but not enough to make a marked difference." Jeff gave a brief nod, jerked his spaniel's lead and headed back to the group of rescuers who had gathered behind him.

"What does this mean? That they're giving up now?" Martin asked, staring off into the distance, his gaze focusing on the lake beside them.

"No, they'll continue. As he said, their task is that much tougher without the scent driving the search. Where did you get out of the car?"

He frowned, turned back to the road and scratched his head. "What? What does that matter?"

"Because the dog might have picked up Adele's scent from the time she got out of the car," the inspector explained.

"I see. Umm... I dropped Louise and the kids off with the picnic stuff and then drove the car to where it was parked earlier."

"Okay, that doesn't match up," Cobbs said thoughtfully.

"What next?" He surveyed the area again, and his gaze was drawn back to the lake once more. "Are you going to search it? The lake?"

Debs sucked in a breath beside him. "No, she can't be in there," she whispered, her voice choked with emotion at the thought.

Inspector Cobbs nodded. "I've just requested the dive team to attend. We wanted to make sure we ruled out the other scenarios first and gave Adele time to resurface, but the time has come to search the lake. I'm sorry if that upsets you, Deborah."

She sniffled. "It's okay. If that's what you need to do, then go ahead and do it. My God, it'll be getting dark soon, won't it?"

They all peered up at the darkening sky, but the inspector shook her head. "We've still got a few hours of daylight ahead of us. It appears darker because of the rain clouds overhead, hopefully they'll move on soon."

Martin glanced at his watch, it was almost six o'clock. "What time will it start getting dark?"

"Around nine to nine-thirty; again, it depends if the rain clouds hamper us or not. Go back to the car, it looks as though another downpour is due any minute. I'll be in touch with you soon."

Martin hooked his arm around Debs' shoulders and guided her back to the car without arguing for a change, his thoughts with his daughter, praying that she hadn't wandered along the water's edge and fallen in. His gaze was drawn further up the shoreline, to see if he could catch a glimpse of the red jumper she'd been wearing that morning, all those hours ago when she went missing. His helplessness increasing with every passing second.

"What are you thinking?" Debs asked, peering over the top of the car and following his gaze.

"I'm not, not really. Oh, all right, I was wondering if she might have headed that way and fell in. She was wearing her red jumper today, I was hoping to see it. Maybe hoping is the wrong word because if I saw it in the water that could only mean one thing, and we really don't want to go down that route, not yet, do we?"

"I'd rather not, no." Debs slipped back into the car. After a final scan of the water's edge, Martin joined her, an uncomfortable nagging twisting at his gut, preventing him from eating any more of his sandwich.

5

$\mathcal{M}$artin and Debs held hands and watched the dive team arrive and begin the process of looking for their daughter. Their mission went on long into the night. At around midnight, Inspector Cobbs approached the car and tapped on the window. Martin jerked his thumb, motioning for her to jump into the back seat.

"Right, just to bring you up to date, they've found nothing so far, which is a good sign, right?" she said as both Debs and Martin turned in their seats to hold a conversation with her.

"Right, I think," Martin replied. "What else are you going to do to help us?"

"Well, a colleague of mine has already spoken to the press back at the station. You might have noticed an extra helicopter flying overhead a few hours ago. That would be the local news reporting from the scene. We asked the media to stay away for the moment; otherwise, it would get too congested up here, and the road is far too narrow to take the stress of a lot of traffic. It's bad enough in the midst of summer out here."

"That's good, isn't it? Has anything come of it so far?" Debs asked.

"Not yet, but we're hopeful."

"What else have you done?" Martin queried, turning back to keep an eye on the dive team.

"I've been busy working in the background. I didn't tell you earlier, but we set up a mini roadblock not long after we arrived, further down the road."

"Why? Oh, God, you really do believe someone took her?" Martin's head swivelled back to the inspector.

"You know it has always been a possibility in my mind, Martin, we needed to rule out all the other options first."

Debs reached for his hand. "Oh my, the thought of someone abducting her... Jesus, I don't know which is worse, fearing she's dead or that someone has abducted her and we will never know what has happened to her or where she is." Tears splattered onto her cheeks, and Martin awkwardly gathered her in his arms across the central console.

"Deborah, we have to keep our hopes alive. We don't know, the blockade proved pointless. I can't offer you anything else, not at this stage. The dive team are about to pack up for the night. I suggest you drive to the hotel down the road; I took the liberty of booking a couple of rooms for you both. There's not much point in you being here any longer."

Martin tore the door open and paced outside. He dipped his head back in the car and shouted, "You're telling us you're giving up on her, aren't you?"

"No. Not in the slightest. I'm saying there's nothing more any of us can do tonight. It's been a long day, everyone's nerves are on edge, I know that. Martin, this is already turning out to be one of the toughest and most frustrating cases I've had to handle, in all honesty. But handle it I will. You have my word that my team and I won't give up until we've found Adele."

"While I admire your indomitable speech, it's not your words that matter to me, to us; it's your actions, Inspector. We appreciate all that you've done so far, but it's resulted in nothing as yet. Our daughter is still out there, terrified out of her mind, whether she has wandered off and got lost in this unforgiving landscape, or God forbid, if someone has taken her. I truly don't know which is worse. If it's the latter scenario, then I'll be praying tonight that whoever has abducted her takes bloody good care of her. The possibility they might drop her off at a paedophile's house…" He turned, bent over and vomited next to the car. He wiped his mouth with the back of his hand. "I'm sorry," he said in a rough voice before continuing, "I don't even want to think about that. All we want is our daughter back."

The inspector stepped out of the car. "I'm aware of that, Martin. Please, I know and appreciate how hard this is on both of you, but you need to give us some time to solve this crime. My sergeant and I are both booked into the hotel as well. We'll grab a few hours' sleep and be back at it first thing in the morning. Take care of each other."

"So you should be. We will."

He watched her walk back to her car and then dropped in beside Debs again. "We might as well call it a day, as she suggested. As much as it grieves me to say, I think she's right."

Debs started the engine. "I agree. We can't see further than the front of the car out here now, anyway, except where it's lit by the dive team. They'll be gone soon enough and then this place will be pitch black."

She set off and followed the inspector up the narrow winding road to the hotel. They all booked in and retired to their rooms. At the door to her room, Debs pleaded with Martin not to leave her.

"Okay, I won't. But no funny business," he warned, breaking into a rare smile.

"I promise. I don't think I could stand being alone, not tonight."

"Me neither." He opened the door and motioned for her to step into the large bay-windowed room. There was a four-poster bed along one wall and a chaise longue along another. He stared at the chaise and mumbled, "I'll take the couch."

Debs laughed. "And have you waking me up when you fall off the edge during the night? No way, we'll share the bed. I'm sure we'll both do our best to resist the temptation to maul each other."

"If you're sure."

"I am. Sleep with your clothes on, if you want to."

"No, I'd rather not, they're still damp. I think I'll take a shower."

"Good idea. Damn, I'll have to rinse my undies out, I drove up here without packing a bag. My head was in such a spin before I got on the road."

"Understandable. I'm sure they'll dry on the heated towel rail or the radiator overnight."

"You shower first and then I'll rinse them out. I don't suppose there are any shops around here anyway."

"Nope, that's a given, we're out in the wilds out here. I think the nearest one is in Seascale." He fell quiet, his train of thought swiftly diverting to that of Adele's safety. "If she's out there, I hope she's all right. I feel guilty being here, tucked up in a cosy hotel room while the temperature outside drops overnight." He sank onto the end of the bed, elbows on his knees, and he covered his head with his hands. "I feel so inadequate, no, worse than that, useless. If only..."

Debs rushed to stand by his side. She touched his hand gently. "You need to stop punishing yourself like this, Martin. It'll soon be daylight again, hold on to that thought."

He looked up at her and smiled. "I'm glad you're here, you were always the one who talked a lot of sense and analysed things logically."

"Ah, they're great traits to have. Come on, it's getting late, go take a shower and I'll climb into bed while you're gone."

Rising from the bed, he paused in front of her and caught the faint smell of her perfume. It smelt comforting and took him back to days gone by, when they'd been together. She grabbed him by the shoulders, pointed him in the direction of the bathroom and patted him on the backside to get him moving.

"Go."

He slipped into the bathroom and closed the door.

Whilst the shower was heating up, he studied his reflection in the mirror over the sink. His eyes were dark underneath and the whites were bloodshot. *It's to be expected, to look an utter mess when one's child is missing, isn't it? Please, please, Adele, be safe and out of harm's way. We'll begin searching again for you at first light and continue searching until we find you.*

The steam hampered his vision, jolting him to strip off and hop in the shower. Tilting his head back, he welcomed the warm spray on his face. Five minutes later, he felt refreshed and invigorated. Maybe it hadn't been the best idea to shower this evening, perhaps he would have been better off leaving it until the morning instead. He dried off and then wrapped the large towel around his middle and returned to the bedroom. Debs was scrolling through her phone.

"What are you doing?" The towel dropped to the floor and he eased into the bed beside her, feeling comfortable in her presence. *Maybe if things were different, we...* Debs' voice brought him back to reality once more.

"I thought I'd check if there was any reaction to the police conference. Looking on Google, it appears to be hot news across all the media sites. If, and it's a big *if*, she's been abducted, maybe putting it out there was a good thing. At least people will be on the lookout for her."

"Hmm... will they?"

"Of course they will. What makes you say that?"

"Oh, I don't know, I have my doubts. Hey, did you supply the inspector with a photo of Adele?"

"No. I never thought. I presumed you had."

"Nope. Is there a photo of her on the internet?"

Debs angled her phone in his direction. "Yes. How did they get hold of it?"

Martin groaned and banged his head several times against the pine headboard. "I bet Louise supplied it. Damn, I've been such a bastard to her."

"Don't blame yourself. I'm sure she'll understand and you'll be able to work things out with her when all this is over."

"Not sure I want to. She probably gave them the photo out of guilt. She's still at fault here, let's not forget that, Debs."

She got out of the bed naked and walked towards the bathroom, her undies in her right hand. "You're a harsh man, Martin. Not forgiving her will eventually eat you up inside."

The door closed behind her, leaving him to contemplate the truth behind her statement. He knew she was right, but refused to back down over such an important issue. Even if they got Adele back, could he ever trust Louise to look after his daughter in the future? He doubted it. As far as he was concerned, there was no way back for them, not in the immediate future, anyway.

He was scrolling through the media attention on Debs' phone when she exited the bathroom. His gaze was drawn to her beautiful curves, the ones his hands used to trace before they split up. During the course of the day, or since her arrival at least, he'd found himself trying to remember how or why they had split up. It was funny how significant facts vanished while the body was under stress.

"Are you spying on me, Martin Jenkins?"

"No, I'm just admiring the perfect view."

She chuckled and pointed at her phone. "I meant that."

"Ugh… sorry, my bad." His cheeks burned.

Debs trotted across the floor to the radiator under the window, spread her underwear out on it, then raced back to the bed and dived under the covers beside him. He was aware they were both naked beneath the duvet and fought hard to control the urge stirring in his groin. *Now is neither the time nor the place, mate. Our kid is missing and all I can think about is…*

Debs reached for the bedside light, turned it on and switched the overhead light off on the wall above the headboard. The intimate lighting only underlined his senses and his dick jumped to attention. He covered the proof by linking his hands together on top of the quilt. "I suppose we'd better try and get some sleep."

Debs leaned over and kissed him on the cheek and then turned her back on him and switched the light off. "Goodnight."

He hunkered down under the quilt, his erection already subsiding. "I hope you sleep well."

"I will, with you beside me."

*H*e managed to drift off, only for a nearby scream to wake him a few hours later.

"Adele! Where are you?" He woke up, shouting.

Disorientated, it took a couple of seconds for him to figure out where he was and what he was doing there. Tearing out of the bed, he switched on the light to find Debs hugging the quilt to her, sobbing. Martin dived back into the bed and gathered her to him. She hesitated at first, went rigid in his arms, but then she quietly relented and allowed his arms to encircle her. Rocking her, he kissed her head over and over. She clung to him. "It's okay. I'm here."

Sniffling, Debs whispered, "Yes, but she's still gone. My baby! My beautiful daughter is missing. I had a nightmare. If I close my eyes again, I know I'll revisit it. I don't want to go there again. Help me, Martin. How do we get over this?"

"There, there. It's a good question, and believe me, I've lain awake most of the night trying to work out where we go from here, but our hands are tied. We need to be patient. We have each other, we're stronger as a unit than we've ever been before. We'll get through this."

"How are we going to do that? It's the unknown that I'm afraid of. I keep putting myself in her position, at least I'm trying to; she must be petrified, scared shitless. I don't know how much more of this I can handle. If we don't find her soon, she could be lost to us forever."

"Honestly, Debs, we truly mustn't go down that route, I won't allow us to write-off our chances of ever being reunited with her."

"I'm sorry. I'm doing my best to remain positive, I promise, but that nightmare… if it comes true, it will completely destroy us."

"You need to put it out of your mind. Nightmares are just the wrong side of your brain coming up with bad scenarios, that's all, sweetheart. Please, don't give it a second thought." He really had no idea if what he was saying was the truth or not. Even to his ears, it sounded dubious, but at this point, he was willing to cling on to anything and everything just to get by.

Debs' sobbing eventually subsided. With her head resting on his chest, she drifted off to sleep. He reached behind him, switched off the main light and laid there, his own mind flitting from one bad notion to another. Surely, nothing good could come out of a situation like this, where a five-year-old goes missing.

With every negative thought that flashed through his mind, his fighting spirit dwindled only for his anger towards Louise to re-emerge. He'd been right to send her packing; there was no way he could be with her, not now, not in the future. To look at her kids enjoying themselves in their rooms would have torn him apart in no time at all.

So why do I feel bad about the way things ended between us? How do I go on from this? Will I ever get my daughter back? Will I ever be able to lead a fulfilling life ever again?

The truth was, there was no way of knowing what lay ahead of them, either of them, or the obstacles they would need to surmount in the days or weeks ahead of them.

Adele, honey, come back to us!

6

*T*he sensation of someone tugging at his arm made him sit bolt upright. "Adele, I'm coming baby. Daddy's coming!"

"I'm sorry to wake you. You were dreaming, saying her name over and over. It was breaking my heart. Oh, Martin, what are we going to do?"

Debs broke down beside him. He gathered her in his arms and ran a soothing hand over her dyed burgundy hair, which was losing its colour at the sides, reverting back to her normal shade of brunette. "We won't know that until we get out there and have a word with the inspector in charge, see if there have been any developments during the night. I'm going to get ready, I suggest you do the same. We'll need to have something to eat before we tackle the day ahead."

"I don't think I could eat anything. My stomach is churning with waves of nausea every time her adorable face enters my mind. I want our daughter back. I can't bear to consider life without her. I won't be able to continue, not without her."

Her despair and the thought of her ending her own life, which is how he'd interpreted what she'd said, knocked him sideways. He tried to remain upbeat when he spoke. "Now what have I told you about remaining positive? Negative thoughts will only have a detrimental effect on your mind and body, don't fall for that trick, hon."

Debs inhaled a shuddering breath and her shoulders shook from the effort. "This is all such a mess. A mess we can't even begin to sift through to find a solution. Our backs are against the wall. It's the inability to correct the issue that is going to eat away at me. I feel numb inside. How do we overcome the helplessness to change the situation?"

"I don't have all the answers, hon. Come on, let's get up and back out there." He eased out from underneath her and threw back the quilt, thankful he hadn't woken up with his usual proud erection.

She said nothing as she watched him cross the room and disappear into the bathroom. When he emerged ten minutes later, he found her glancing out of the window at the surrounding hills, the quilt wrapped around her.

"The bathroom is free, are you all right?"

"It's a beautiful area. Enticing for a child to explore, if that's what happened."

"I'd rather think that than the alternative. I regret coming here, we should have gone to the beach instead. Had we done that yesterday morning, we wouldn't be dealing with this situation right now."

"There's no point thinking like that, Martin, we have to accept it and move on. I'll get dressed. If you want to go down for breakfast, I'll catch up with you."

"Are you going to eat something?"

She shrugged. "Maybe I'll force a bowl of cereal down me, nothing more."

She waddled across the room and dropped the quilt on the floor once she reached the bathroom door. He fetched it and threw it on the bed, then left the room. In the corridor, he found the sergeant about to knock on one of the bedroom doors. He turned to look at Martin and offered an awkward smile.

"Morning, how are things?"

Martin nodded. "I was about to ask the same. Any news?"

"I'm sorry, no."

The door opened, and the inspector came out of the room. "Good morning, Martin. Did you sleep well?"

"What do you think?" he retorted harshly. "Sorry, I didn't mean for it to come out like that. Off and on. You?"

"Yes and no. I spent most of the night checking the internet and ringing the station for updates. Nothing new to report. Are you going down for breakfast?"

"Yes, just on my way." He jabbed a thumb behind him and said, "Debs is taking a shower. She'll join me in a few minutes. I've persuaded her to have a bowl of cereal at least."

"Very wise. Join us, we can discuss where we go from here, if you're up for that first thing in the morning?"

"Yes, I'm eager to hear what your thoughts are."

The three of them walked the length of the corridor and descended the stairs. A young blonde waitress was waiting at the entrance of the dining room. She smiled and said, "Good morning. I hope you slept well." Not bothering to wait for a response, she went on, "Please help yourselves to cereal, continental breakfast and juice. I'll be over shortly to take your order for a cooked breakfast, should you want one, and any drinks you require."

"Thanks very much," the inspector replied, speaking on behalf of all of them.

Cobbs and Jones made their way over to a table situated in the bay window while Martin made a detour and chose muesli, a pain au chocolat and a small glass of orange juice from the display on offer.

Uneasily, he sat down opposite the detectives. Guilt seeping through him, he offered, "Lack of food throughout the day yesterday, thought I'd make up for it today instead."

"No need to explain. It's a great idea to keep your strength up," the inspector agreed as the waitress appeared beside her.

"What would you like? Tea or coffee?"

"Coffee for me," Martin was the first to respond.

"Two coffees, thanks. Bob, what do you fancy?" the inspector asked her partner.

His reply was an awkward one. "Would a full-English be all right, boss?"

"Of course. Martin?"

"Yes, that'll be great for me too."

"What about Deborah, what do you think she'll want when she joins us?"

"A bowl of cereal, that's all."

Cobbs nodded. "Okay, and I'll have scrambled eggs on toast with some crispy bacon on the side, if that's all right?"

"Okey dokey. I'll be back shortly with your drinks and some toast." The waitress dashed to the other side of the room and went into the kitchen.

"The staff are efficient, hopefully we won't be kept waiting too long," Cobbs announced.

Martin tucked into his cereal, his stomach growling in complaint at being forgotten about the previous day. He looked down at it. "It's coming, be patient."

The inspector smiled. "How's Debs this morning?"

He paused before shovelling in another spoonful. "She seems okay, we both are. Are the Mountain Rescue Team going to join us again this morning? What's the plan?"

"Yes, I've asked each of the teams to rejoin us, well, all except the dive team, that is. There's no point in them coming all the way out here again."

"It was a relief to see them draw a blank, even though it hasn't solved the mystery of Adele's disappearance as yet."

"Agreed. They were relieved not to discover her body in the lake as well, from what I can gather."

"You said you'd been in touch with the station during the night, anything from that?" Martin studied her as he sipped his orange juice.

"Nothing so far. With any case similar to this, we have to sift through the calls we receive; some are more valuable than others shall we say, especially when a child disappears."

Martin glanced up from his breakfast and frowned. "Don't tell me there are folks out there who deliberately try and put the police off the scent early on in the investigation."

Cobbs smiled. "All right, I won't, but the opposite is the truth. There are certain sectors of our society which tend to band together at moments like this and set out to cause mischief."

Martin paused and thought the prospect over for a second or two before the penny finally dropped. "No, you're talking about paedos, right?"

"Yes, unfortunately. Once word gets out, they'll do anything and everything to get in our way."

"Bloody hell, I've never even considered that possibility before."

"It makes our job so much tougher, which is their intention."

"Do you think they send messages to each other, to ensure everything goes according to plan? I can't believe I'm thinking this deviously, let alone discussing it with you."

"Yes, on the Dark Web, anything is possible to achieve. It drives an SIO, like me, crazy most of the time."

"I can imagine. Makes your job a thousand times worse as well, right?"

"Absolutely. Not every family member involved in a case understands the trials and tribulations laid out before us. If Adele has been abducted… let's just say, our job is never going to be easy, from the outset."

"What's that?" Debs asked, joining them at the table. "Morning, by the way."

The inspector smiled. "How are you? Or is that a particularly silly question?"

"Before you answer that," Martin butted in, "what cereal do you want?"

Debs leaned over and peered into his bowl. "That looks fine to me."

He shoved back his chair and collected a bowl, filled it with muesli and picked up a glass of pineapple instead of orange juice. He placed her breakfast in front of her and retook his seat.

Debs covered his hand with hers. "You remembered how much I detest orange juice, I'm touched."

His cheeks warmed under the inspector's scrutiny. "We were just discussing what lies ahead of us today."

Debs glanced at Cobbs. "To answer your question, Inspector, I'm not totally sure I can supply an adequate answer. I had a nightmare during the night. I'd rather not say what it consisted of, I'll leave that to your imagination. Where do we go from here?"

The inspector nodded her understanding. "We continue the search out here, at least until lunchtime, and assess which way we go from there. In the meantime, we'll be sifting through the dozens of calls we've received back at the station to see if there are any leads worth following up on."

Debs dropped her spoon. "That's brilliant news. Has anyone said they've actually seen Adele?"

The inspector bowed her head for a moment and then looked Debs in the eye and replied, "Plenty, as I was explaining to Martin before you arrived, the Dark Web has a lot to answer for at times like this."

Debs' head swivelled between the three of them. "What am I missing here?"

"Paedos band together, love, try to send the police on a different path."

Debs shook her head and tears welled up in her striking green eyes. "My God, can this be true? What are you saying? That once a child goes missing the likelihood of them ever being found is...? I don't want to say what I'm thinking."

"That's where your faith must play a part," the inspector stated. "Our job is a difficult one from the start; it escalates to a different level once word gets out in the media. There are some extremely twisted people in the world today." As soon as the words were aired, Cobbs winced. "I'm not telling you anything new when I say that, am I?"

"No," Martin admitted. "But thinking and knowing are entirely different things."

"I have to add a note of caution you need to consider in these types of cases. When a child is abducted, the perpetrator usually has an agenda and is often an opportunist. I want to assure you, however, that just because Adele may have been taken doesn't mean to say that any harm will come to her."

"But you can't assure us that'll be the case either," Martin replied.

The waitress appeared with the cooked food order and put the plates in front of them, then returned to the kitchen to fetch their drinks.

In the interim, the table remained quiet, each of them lost in their own thoughts. After the waitress delivered the drinks and took Debs' order for a coffee, she returned to the kitchen.

The inspector waited until the waitress was out of earshot before she said, "Until we have actual evidence at our disposal, everything I've suggested is pure speculation; maybe we should leave that particular conversation there."

The waitress deposited Debs' coffee and left them to it once more. The table remained quiet, the only noise to be heard was the clinking of cutlery on the plates as the four of them tucked into their breakfasts.

Not long after, Debs pushed her half-eaten cereal away.

"You should eat more than that, Debs," Martin suggested.

"I can't. I have a lump in my chest that's the size of a bloody watermelon, it's a struggle to get anything down. I'll be fine, I've had enough for now." She sat back and glanced out of the window at the cars leaving the hotel. "Have you searched all the cars in the area? What if Adele is in the boot of one of those?"

"I doubt it, Deborah," the inspector said. "Whoever took her, if that's the case, I think we can safely assume that they would have left the area yesterday, soon after she went missing."

Martin frowned. "If you believe that, why are you continuing the search?"

Smiling, she told them, "I've been known to be wrong in the past, not often, admittedly, but this way, I'm covering all the bases."

A disturbance at the entrance of the dining room caught their attention. The inspector groaned, wiped the grease off her mouth on a serviette and crossed the room to address the issue. The room wasn't that large, so they could just about hear what was being said.

"Gents, what did I tell you earlier? Give us, and the parents, the space we need, will you? I appreciate you coming out here and reporting on the missing child, but I reiterate, do not hound the parents, or I'll come down heavily on you."

"Hey, come on, Inspector, let us have a brief chat with them. The public have a right to know what they're going through at a time like this."

"I'm sure the general public have enough savvy to appreciate the anxiety the couple are dealing with. I can't allow it."

Martin left his chair and raced over to join the inspector; the sergeant tried his best to prevent him but failed.

"Why are you hounding us at a time like this?" Martin demanded. His question was aimed at the tall, skinny man with the large nose standing ahead of the surging pack, who appeared to be the group's spokesperson.

"We're not, mate. The public can be a great help during instances like this. Why not do us all a favour and give us a heartfelt interview? You could make a personal plea to the kidnappers, if that's what happened to your little girl. It'll make you feel better, I promise, you know, knowing that you reached out for your child through the media. Go on, what do you say?"

Unsure, Martin looked at Cobbs for guidance. "What do you think?"

"It's up to you. I've known interviews with the press being beneficial in the past, but they can also take a lot out of the parents at the same time."

"But if it's a means to get to Adele and whoever has taken her, I think I'm willing to take the risk."

The journalist gave him a smug smile. "Good man. I'll get things set up and get back to you in ten minutes, give you time to finish off your breakfast. What's your name?"

"Martin Jenkins."

The inspector wagged a finger at the journalist. "One word out of line and I'll throw the bloody book at you. This is about the parents and Adele, got that? Don't use this interview as an ego boost for yourself to further advance your career. Am I making myself clear, Roberts?"

The reporter grinned broadly. "Crystal. He'll be safe in my hands, you should know that, Inspector. I'll be back soon to collect you, Mr Jenkins." He strained his neck and looked over at the breakfast table. "Will your wife be joining us? It'll make more of an impact if both of you speak."

"No. Leave her out of it." Martin walked back to the table and explained to Debs what was about to happen. "I told him it'll just be me talking, is that all right?"

"God, yes. I'd be a nervous wreck and get all tongue-tied if he asked me any questions, anyway."

The inspector retook her seat. She frowned, letting Martin know she'd thought he'd overstepped the mark.

He felt the need to apologise. "I'm sorry I butted in like that."

"It's okay. I wish you luck with the interview. A word of warning, if I may?" Martin nodded. "Refuse to answer, or dodge any questions that you feel uncomfortable answering. He's one of the cannier journalists; once he gets an idea in his head, he keeps chipping away until he gets a suitable answer. Just be aware of that, don't take any shit, but also be aware that he'll try to twist you into knots to gain what he believes is the truth. Did that make any sense?"

"Yes, shit. I'm regretting giving him the go-ahead now. Me and my big mouth. My intentions were good."

"In one way, I think it's a good idea to hold the interview. If it were up to me, it wouldn't have taken place so soon, but we need to look on the positive side and believe it can help us bring Adele back."

"I'm confused," Debs said. "How can talking to the press harm our cause?"

"Invariably, it doesn't; but occasionally, it can. I'm sorry, I don't want to put a dampener on things, I'm just adding a word of caution, that's all."

"Would it be a cheek if I asked you to be by my side during the interview, Inspector?"

"I... umm, I have the troops to rally first, Martin. I wasn't expecting anything else to crop up and have asked the team to assemble in ten minutes, around the time of the interview. So regrettably, I'm going to have to decline and tell you, you're on your own on this one."

His head sank and Debs covered his hand with hers. "You've got this, Martin. Do you want me to join you for moral support?"

"No. I'd rather keep you out of the limelight, if that's okay, Debs."

"It's your call."

"I agree with Martin," the inspector said. "I think he's strong enough to handle the type of probing questions Roberts prefers to ask."

"Damn, what have I done?" Martin ran a hand through his hair and stared out of the window at the pack of journalists all chatting away, some of them more animated than others.

"Hey, just answer the questions you feel comfortable with and go from there. Okay?" Cobbs said. Her smile was a forgiving one, considering the predicament he'd put them both in.

"I need another coffee if I'm going to deal with that lot."

Cobbs clicked her fingers to summon the waitress. "Coffees all round, please, if you don't mind?"

"I'll be right back. Thank you for sorting the journalists out for me," the waitress replied, sheepishly.

"Not a problem. If they get too much, just give us a shout and we'll instruct them to back off."

"Thanks. I'll be back with your drinks soon."

The waitress left and another awkward silence descended until Martin heaved out a sigh. "Is there anything I shouldn't say? If you can give me some guidance there."

"Not really. Just tell them we're covering a few possibilities. At the end of the day, everything is a supposition up to this point, you know that. We could step outside, begin the search and find Adele cowering in a spot we checked yesterday, who knows?"

Debs squeezed his hand. "Let's hope that's the case. I just thought as the word had got out last night, it would be best to talk to the press sooner rather than later. Keeping Adele's image in the mind of the public will help our cause in the long run, won't it?" Martin said.

"You're right to think that, which is why we put an alert out last night. I hate that you've been forced to speak to the reporter at this early stage, you know, with your emotions being fraught. I tend to try and protect families a little longer."

"So they get used to the idea of their child going missing, is that what you're saying?"

Inspector Cobbs shrugged. "Maybe. It's never good to rush these things, but what's done is done."

"You want me to call the interview off?" he asked, doubts seeping into his mind.

"No, it'll look bad if you do that now. You need to keep the reporters on your side, working for us. Piss them off and they could switch just like that." The inspector clicked her fingers.

"By that you mean they could start reporting that we've done something to our child? Correction, that *I've* done something to Adele?"

"Possibly, it's always wise to remain friendly with them throughout an interview."

Martin groaned. "Thanks for the warning." He peered at the kitchen door just as it opened. "Boy, do I need that extra cup of caffeine."

The waitress deposited the cups and cleared away the plates of half-eaten food.

He popped two sugar cubes in his cup and stirred it. Debs leaned in and asked, "Are you sure about this?"

"Er, no... but I figure it can't hurt. The more people out there looking for Adele the better, yes?"

She smiled and nodded. "I suppose so. Be careful."

"I will. Drink up."

$\mathcal{R}$oberts, the reporter, was actually quite gentle and easy-going with his questions, not intrusive as Martin had feared. He came away from the interview relieved that it had gone so well.

Debs was congratulating Martin as the journalists dispersed outside the hotel. A car drew up alongside them and Louise stepped out. A pang of guilt tore at his insides.

"Martin."

He took a step away from Debs and approached the vehicle. "Louise. I thought you left yesterday."

"No. I decided to go back today, we were all exhausted after what went on yesterday. I expected you back last night."

"The inspector booked a room for me here. I didn't get to bed until gone one, after the dive team left."

She gasped and turned to look at the lake. "Did they find anything?"

"No. Which we're taking to be a positive outcome; at least we have hope she's still alive."

Louise looked at him again and nodded. "Any other news?"

"Not really. I've just held a press conference with the journalists. The inspector seems to think Adele was abducted."

Another gasp. "Oh, God, not that. I'm so sorry."

"Yes, you said as much yesterday." His blood scorched his veins and he struggled to prevent the anger from revealing itself in his tone.

Louise seemed shocked by the sudden change in him. "I can't keep saying it, Martin. I've barely slept all night as it is."

"Yeah, you and me both. Go home, Louise."

"I'm going. Thanks for letting me use the car."

"It's okay. Debs is here, she'll give me a lift back to Liverpool."

Louise glanced past him at Deborah. She threw him the keys of the cottage and slipped behind the steering wheel without saying another word.

He took a step back and watched Louise and her kids drive away. Debs hooked an arm through his. "Don't be too hard on her, Martin. You can see what pain she's going through."

He shook his head. "Not enough. She shouldn't have let our daughter wander off, end of."

"I know. But punishing her for something that was out of her control isn't going to help matters, is it?"

"I know you're right. However, every time I see her, the anger starts to build again. Anyway, enough about them, they've gone. What do you think we should do now?"

"Sit and wait, I suppose, as the inspector suggested. There's really nothing else we can do at the moment."

The wind picked up. "Okay, let's go back inside in case it rains. After an hour or so, I'll come back out and chase up the inspector to see how things are progressing. That is if I don't go out of my mind in the interim."

"Did the reporters tell you when they'll be airing the interview?"

"Lunchtime at the earliest."

"That's a shame. I thought it might go out in the morning news bulletin. It's the waiting around that is going to kill us."

"Well, we could always go back to the cottage. I need to pack up my stuff and return the keys to the owner, anyway."

"Good idea. Shall we go now?"

"Why not? I'm going to tell the inspector what we're up to. I'll be back in a sec."

"I'll be waiting in the car."

He jogged across the car park to where the inspector was instructing the uniformed coppers who had just arrived. She saw him coming and wrapped things up as he reached her. "Go, people, ask your questions and start the search all over again. Give me a shout if you find anything at all." She turned to face him. "How did it go with the reporters?"

"Yeah, it was fine in the end. I think they felt sorry enough for me not to badger me too much. Just wanted to let you know that Debs and I are going back to the cottage to pick up my belongings. Louise dropped by with the keys, not five minutes ago."

"I saw her. Is she heading back to Liverpool now?"

"Yes. Good riddance, I say."

Cobbs raised an eyebrow. "You're going to have to forgive her one day. These things happen, Martin, no one is to blame."

"I have a different take on it, Inspector. I was watching her child like a hawk, I expected her to do the same, especially in a strange area."

"We're never going to agree on that one. I think Louise is feeling guilty enough as it is, without you heaping more blame on her. That's my take, anyway."

"You're entitled to your opinion, as am I. We'll be back soon."

He spun on his heel, seething, and returned to the car park where Debs was waiting for him. He jumped in the car and they set off, winding their way through the nearby cars parked at odd angles along the narrow road that led back to the lake. "I think we should go back. Take the long way around."

Debs agreed and began a three-point turn that actually turned out to take five attempts. "It's narrower than I thought, nothing wrong with my driving, just in case you were debating whether to have a go at me."

He placed a hand over his chest. "Moi? I wouldn't dream of criticising your wonderful driving skills."

"Yeah, right," she muttered, putting her foot down.

*T*hey pulled up outside the cottage around thirty minutes later. His heart pounded at the prospect of having to pack up his and Adele's things. He hesitated on the threshold of the cottage until Debs nudged his elbow.

"Come on, get in, the wind is picking up and it's getting chilly."

"It's just that… you're right, I'm being foolish. Okay." He opened the front door and stood back to allow Debs to enter the cottage first.

"Wow, this is lovely. Hey, you never brought me to anywhere as special as this when we were together."

"Sorry. It wasn't really my idea. At least, I don't think it was. To be honest, I can't remember whose idea it was to book this place. I regret doing it now though, after what's occurred."

"It's no good having regrets, Martin. You need to get past how it happened or how you could have prevented it, you should move on. I don't mean for you to forget about our baby or that she is out there… missing, but you should let go the cause of her disappearance. Otherwise, it's going to become a burden that will end up blighting your life."

Martin nodded. "I hear you. It's so hard, though." He rubbed his face. "Okay, let's go upstairs."

Debs peered into the small downstairs rooms and caught his arm as he passed her in the hallway. "There's a note on the kitchen table."

"I'll get it on the way down." He continued on his journey up the creaking, narrow staircase to the master bedroom where Adele's pretty pink suitcase was lying on the bed. He sucked in a steadying breath and walked towards it. Louise had packed his daughter's belongings for him. Tears misted his vision. He checked the small wardrobe and all the drawers in the room to ensure nothing had been missed. Then he got down on all fours and checked under the bed. His heart almost stopped. There, sitting upright, against the wall, was his daughter's doll, the one she loved and preferred to take to bed with her at night. He pulled it towards him and cradled it in his arms.

Debs arrived in the doorway and sniffled. "Lucy Lou, she never goes anywhere without that doll."

He whimpered. "She didn't take it with her when we went to Wast Water, why? It looks as though it's been placed here for us to find."

Debs wiped away the stream of tears cascading down her cheeks. "I don't know."

Martin's devious mind went into overdrive. *Did Louise do it? Intentionally place the doll there, in the hope that he would find it? How callous of her, if she had.*

"What is it? I know when you're thinking something, spit it out."

"It's as though someone was intentionally goading me, us, by placing the doll there. Her treasured companion."

"No, you're wrong. That's... unthinkable, I refuse to even consider it. I just can't, Martin."

"I'm sorry, Debs. The truth always hurts in situations like this. I stick by what I said."

"Louise? You think she did this? I don't want to believe another mother could be that cold-hearted."

"Either Louise or one of her kids."

Debs shook her head vigorously. "No, you have to be wrong. I bet Adele placed the doll there in the morning before she left. It's the type of thing she used to do, sorry, she does. Line all her teddies and dolls up when she's not playing with them. Don't think badly of people just because something doesn't feel right to you, Martin."

"Oh, I don't know. What I do know is that I failed my daughter. I don't know her as well as I should."

Debs hugged him. "If you're feeling guilty about that, then I should be partially to blame as well."

He squeezed her and rested his chin on top of her head. "What's the point... in any of this? Like you said, the bitterness will only end up eating away at me. It's so hard not to be angry, knowing that Adele is out of our grasp and that something bad could have happened to her."

At that moment, his mobile rang. He pushed Debs away and groaned when he noted the name on the screen. "It's Morgan."

Debs wrinkled her nose. "You'd better answer it, she's not the type to give up if you don't. I'll go downstairs, leave you to it."

Martin smiled. Debs and his sister, Morgan, had never really got on in the past. "Hello, Morgan."

"Why didn't you ring me? I've just seen the story running on the news."

"I've been a little preoccupied, as you can imagine."

"My God, that poor child. Any news yet? Are the police there?"

"No news and, yes, of course the police are here. Plus the Mountain Rescue Team, also the dive team, and no, no one has found her yet." The more he relayed, the more it affected him. He was on the verge of tears, trying to hold it together.

"There's no need for you to snap at me, Martin. I've taken the trouble to call you, the least you can do is keep a civil tongue in your head."

"Get off your high horse, Morgan. I don't need this shit from you."

"I'm not flinging any *shit*, all I'm asking is for an update on my niece's whereabouts."

"What? The niece you've barely spoken to since she was born?"

"Bollocks. There's no talking to you at times. You drove this family apart, you'd be wise to remember that, Martin. I'm trying to make amends here, although why I'm bothering is bloody beyond me."

"Morgan, two words: FUCK OFF!" He jabbed his finger at the *End Call* button, picked up Lucy Lou and Adele's case and went into the other bedroom to pack his case, only to find Louise had done it for him. After checking that nothing had been left behind in the drawers, he descended the stairs to find Debs standing at the bottom, open-mouthed. "What? You heard? She deserved it. I can't be dealing with people coming out of the woodwork like that and having a go at me. I'm well aware that her getting in touch will lead her to blaming me, eventually."

"I know things have always been tense between you, but maybe you should cut her some slack; perhaps, this was her way of trying to make amends for not getting in touch."

Sighing, he nodded. "Possibly. I'll ring her back once things have settled down a bit. I'm not in the mood to listen to her condescension right now. Are you ready to go?"

"Yes, but you're forgetting one thing… the note."

After placing the cases on the floor, he walked into the kitchen and opened the sheet of paper which had been folded in half and read it.

Martin,

You probably won't want to read this at this terrible time, but I wanted to reiterate how sorry I am. Had I known this would happen, I would have undoubtedly kept a closer eye on Adele.

I get that you hate me right now, I don't blame you. But I swear to you, you can't possibly hate me more than I hate myself.

I hope, eventually, that you will be able to find it in your heart to forgive me. And most of all, I hope we can overcome this one day and possibly pick up where we left off.

Always remember the good times we've shared over the past few months and how much I love you.

You mean everything to me and more.

Love you always,

Louise.

His stomach somersaulted, but his heart remained hardened to the words. That's all they were, after all. *If she'd loved me, she would have taken better care of my daughter. How can I possibly forgive such incompetence?* He drifted back into the hallway and smiled at Debs. "It was nothing worth sharing. Only Louise having the audacity to plead for forgiveness."

"I'm in a difficult position; I know she broke up our family in the first place by having an affair with you, but when I saw her earlier, she looked distraught, love. Maybe you should truly think things over where she's concerned. Don't let it fester before you speak to her again."

He kissed the top of her head and whispered, "I know who I want, and it's not her. Are you ready?"

Shocked, Debs nodded and walked back outside. Martin followed her out and paused. On the horizon, he could see the hills which framed Wast Water; their bleakness seemed to be drawing him back there.

Debs still hadn't spoken, she got in the passenger seat beside him and secured her seatbelt.

"Everything all right?" he tentatively asked.

"I don't know, is it?"

He shrugged. "Let's talk about it another time. I'm desperate to get back there. I need to drop the keys off first, it's only up the road."

Debs only said one word: "Okay."

He called ahead to make the arrangements. The owner's house was five minutes away. Martin exited the car and handed the keys to the woman who was standing at the gate to meet him. "Sorry we couldn't stay; in the circumstances, I'm sure you'll understand."

"Of course. I'm so very sorry this happened to your family. Is there any news? Have the police any idea how she went missing?"

"Not yet, well, maybe. They're now thinking along the lines that Adele has possibly been abducted."

The woman held her hand up to her cheek. "Oh my, that's simply awful. Who would do such a thing in this beautiful area?"

"That's what we're hoping to find out. I have to go. Thanks for everything."

"Don't mention it. I'd normally say I hope to see you again in the near future, but I doubt you'll want to return to this area again."

"I think you're right, not unless it's to pick my baby up. Thanks again." He ran back to the car and pulled away. As he drove off, he watched the woman wave and then go back inside the house.

After a few minutes of silence, Debs muttered, "She seemed nice."

"Yes. She was cut up about Adele. I couldn't stick around for long,

I felt like she was going to bombard me with uncomfortable questions."

"It's human nature to be interested when something like this occurs, I suppose."

"I wouldn't sink to that level, if someone else was having to contend with this shit."

"Everyone is different, you know that."

"True enough." Rain splattered the windscreen in big blobs. "Jesus, just what we don't need."

"Will it hamper the search?"

"It shouldn't do. Isn't that what this area is renowned for? Wet weather... the locals should be used to it."

"Let's hope you're right. I hope they soon find out what's happened to Adele."

"Here's hoping."

They were almost back at the search site when Martin's mobile rang for the second time that morning. He pulled over to take the call, preferring to check the ID before he accepted it on the hands-free. He groaned and bashed his hand on the steering wheel. "What the heck does she want?"

"Who?"

"My damn mother. I haven't spoken to her since we split up."

"I didn't know that. Maybe your sister rang her to complain about you."

Martin pointed a finger. "I bet you're right. Should I answer it or ignore her?"

"How do you feel about talking to her?"

"I don't know. The last thing I want, or need, at this moment is for her to pull me over the damn coals for telling Morgan to fuck off."

"You don't know that's going to happen, not until you take the call. I'll be here to support you."

"You're a good woman, Debs. Okay, here goes." He pressed the button to accept the call and placed it on speaker, so they could both hear. "Hello, Mother. How are you?"

"Fine. How are you? And before you ask, yes, Morgan called me and told me about the conversation she had with you earlier."

He rolled his eyes. "And what, you decided to heap on the pressure by calling me to have your say on the issue, is that it?"

"No, not at all. We're only trying to help, Martin. Adele is our flesh and blood too, you know."

"Yeah, and I'm your son, you know, the one you saw fit to ignore all these months since Debs and I broke up. How does that work, eh, Mum?"

"I'm sorry. I've been really busy trying to keep the salon afloat. I saw you on TV, you look older."

He held his palms upright and stared at Debs in disbelief. "What do you expect me to say to that? I'm living through hell on earth and that's the first thing that comes out of your damn mouth."

"I'm sorry. Don't use that tone with me or I'll hang up. All your sister and I are trying to do is reach out to lend you our support."

"Mother, it's the way you confront me within a few sentences that I can't handle. Why would you both do that, knowing the stress and anxiety I'm dealing with at present? It doesn't make sense. This situation is about my daughter and yet the pair of you have instantly gone on the attack with your verbal diarrhoea. Believe me, I neither want nor need it. Now if that's all, I'd prefer to be out there searching for my darling daughter than wasting time arguing the toss with you about what tone of voice I'm bloody using."

"Wait! Don't you dare hang up on me. I have a right to know what's going on. What are the police doing about Adele?"

"Ya think? After turning your back on me for months on end, when I've been at my lowest ebb some days... you've got a frigging nerve. I'll ring you, if we ever find her. Until such a day, leave me alone. That goes for Morgan as well. I can do without all your self-righteous attitude, especially when my daughter is missing." He ended the call, rested his head back and released a growl through gritted teeth. "Can you effing believe it? Jesus, what have I ever done in this life to have such a detestable mother who thinks she's in the right all the time?"

Debs placed a hand on his arm. "I think you're blowing this up out of all proportion, sweetie."

"Really? Didn't you just hear what she said?"

"I heard a mother reaching out to her son and you taking things the wrong way."

"I did?"

"It doesn't matter now. I think we need to get back to make Adele our priority and worry about how you deal with Morgan and your mother once we've found her. Deal?"

"If you say so. Although I have to tell you, their annoying criticism is going to niggle away at me for a while."

Debs smiled and nodded. "I understand. Come on."

Martin pushed the phone call aside and concentrated on what they needed to do to get Adele back. If only he knew the answer to that particular conundrum. He continued along the narrow road to the area where he and Louise had chosen to have a picnic the day before, to find an excess of cars at the location. Off to one side was a group of journalists with mics in their hands, trying to speak to some of the rescuers and the individuals who were gathered. "Jesus, wouldn't you have thought the police would have sealed off this area? Why is the road still open?"

"Makes you wonder. Maybe you should ask the inspector that."

He slotted the car into neutral, applied the handbrake and shot out of the vehicle, leaving Debs behind. His anger bubbling to the surface, he strode towards the inspector who was talking to someone on the phone. He hung back a little, to eavesdrop on her conversation. It was impossible to glean what was being said because Cobbs was only answering with a yes or no. She smiled and held up a finger, letting him know that she wouldn't be a moment. Eventually, she ended the call. By that time, Martin was soaked through for the second day on the trot. The inspector was bone dry, using the large umbrella to shield her from the elements.

"Hello, Martin. What can I do for you?"

He took a few steps forward. "For a start, you can tell me why you haven't closed off the road to this area."

"It wouldn't make sense to do that. The teams need to have access to this spot in order to carry out the searches."

"What about evidence? The fact you believe she may have been abducted? Therefore, the more people trampling around here, the less chance there will be for us to obtain any worthwhile evidence, and that will hamper our case, won't it?" His desperation notched up another level. He knew he was clutching at straws but he couldn't stand around and say nothing.

"We handled that side of things yesterday, you're aware of that. Why are you questioning the way I'm doing my job?"

Martin paced back and forth a few times and shook his head. "I'm sorry. I feel so inadequate, I'm just trying to piece things together in my head. Sorting out what I believe is right and wrong and coming up with dumb outcomes."

"It's okay. Why don't you and Deborah go back to the hotel, out of the rain? There's nothing more you can do out here, not today."

"Any news from the media slots?" he asked, more out of hope than expectation.

"Not yet. Not of any relevance so far."

"Are you continuing to get hoax calls?"

Cobbs sighed. "Unfortunately, it's taking a while for my team to sift through them."

"Bastards. How can people be so damned heartless when a family is going through a situation of this magnitude?"

"It's beyond me at times."

"I'm glad you're still taking the investigation seriously." He glanced around him, at the number of police within spitting distance of where they were standing.

"They'll be here until one o'clock. Then…" her voice trailed off.

He quickly turned to face her again and asked, "Then? Don't tell me you'll be giving up on us?"

"Regrettably, yes. We have to, if nothing shows up this morning."

"Why? It's not long enough. My daughter is missing. She could be out there, dying from exposure for all we know. Please, won't you reconsider?"

"The longer the situation goes on with the lack of clues, the more I believe she was abducted. If that's the case, then all we're doing by keeping a presence here is delaying our work elsewhere."

He sighed heavily. "So you're not telling me you're throwing in the towel completely?"

"Far from it. I assure you. I won't give up until Adele is back with you and her mother."

"Well, that's a relief. Okay, I'll let you get on. We'll be at the hotel."

Cobbs looked him up and down. "Good, have you got a change of clothes?"

"Yes, we've just collected my things from the cottage."

"Good idea. Once we leave here at lunchtime, will you be heading back to Liverpool?"

"We'll need guidance on what to do next, if you have the time to go through things with us."

"Of course. I'll come and find you later."

Dejected, his head hung low, Martin made his way back to the car and then drove to the hotel. After getting changed, he and Debs sat in the bay window of the lounge area, watching all that was going on around them while keeping a careful eye on the clock. Lunchtime soon crept up on them.

"Do you want something to eat?" Debs asked.

"Maybe a sandwich, I don't think I could stomach much."

"Me neither. What about we share a sandwich and ask if they'll do us a bowl of chips, just to make sure we have something hot inside us? Who knows when we'll be eating again, if we need to get on the road later?"

"Good idea." He reached for her hand. She slipped hers into his and he squeezed it tightly. "I'm glad you're here with me. I'd be a lost cause without you."

"Nonsense, you're stronger than you think. I'll place the order." She stood and touched a hand to his cheek, the way she used to do when they were married. It felt comforting to feel her touch, and tears dampened his eyes. Not for the first time, he found himself wondering how their once solid relationship had ended. He watched her walk away, and images of her carrying Adele as a bump swept through his mind. Not being able to stand the heartrending emotions a moment longer, his gaze returned to the dwindling activity going on outside. Finally, the media were packing up and leaving. His heart sank at the realisation that the police wouldn't be far behind them.

"Everything all right?" Debs asked, placing two bundles of cutlery on the table along with vinegar and ketchup.

"You remembered." He smiled, gesturing to the condiments.

"Of course, it hasn't been that long since you were in my life."

He was silent while he collected his thoughts. "I have so many regrets in this life, the biggest being leaving you and our child."

"You say that now, only because of the situation we're in. You left because you were unhappy."

"Not true. I thought I was. My dick did the talking for me. Sorry to be so crude, but it's the truth. I still loved you, right up to the day I packed my stuff and gave you back the keys to the house." Debs glanced down at her lap. He couldn't tell if she was embarrassed by his confession or whether she was trying to avoid the subject. He reached for her hand. "Speak to me."

She looked up, and he saw the sadness in her eyes and the tears forming. "You broke my heart that day. I didn't think I'd ever be able to forgive you, but here we are, supporting each other in a desperate attempt to get through this horrendous ordeal."

"I'll forever be grateful to you for coming here, to be with me. The way you've reacted has put me to shame. Many women would have come here wielding a knife if their ex had 'lost their child', but not you. You accepted it for the disaster it was and have forgiven me. At least, that's how I'm reading it."

"There was never anything to forgive, Martin. I could see the torment you were going through. The last thing you needed was me heaping more guilt on you. Anyway, you weren't to blame, not directly, not if you weren't there, although…"

"Go on, say it. I need to feel your anger, so far you haven't shown much emotion. It's good to get it out, sweetheart, believe me."

"Haven't shown much emotion? Are you kidding me? I'm gutted, as much as you are, if not more. I've taken a step back and realised there's no point in ranting and raving at you or anyone else, what use would it be in the long run? I'm aware of how much you love Adele, going through the court system reinforced that. Please, let's not go over old ground here. I really don't see the point. Our priority remains to get our daughter back home. What happens after we've achieved that, well… let's cross that bridge later, eh?"

"Are you telling me there's hope for us in the future? Despite me letting you and Adele down?" His heart skipped around in his chest doing a happy dance at the prospect of getting back together with Debs and Adele, once she came home. If she came home.

"They say you should never go back, but I don't believe that's true. I think everyone deserves a second chance in this life. I've never stopped loving you, Martin."

Taken aback, he stared at her for a while and then leaned over and their lips met in the lightest of kisses.

A cough behind them broke them apart. He looked back to find Inspector Cobbs standing there with Sergeant Jones. He leapt out of his seat, embarrassed they'd been caught out. "Have you found something?" He wiped the sweat from his palms on his jeans.

"I've come to tell you that a nearby police force is staking out a house at present, following a lead from the public."

"My God. Do they believe Adele is inside? They must do, right? Dumb question."

"We need you to remain calm, Martin, Deborah. The general public, in their eagerness to reach out and help, can often be wrong in cases such as this."

"What are they going to do? Why don't they burst in there?"

"I've just explained why, Martin, we have to be cautious. I've sent a photo of Adele, let's sit tight and see how that pans out, okay?"

"Thank you, Inspector," Debs replied. She tugged on Martin's arm to make him sit down again. "Let's have some faith, Martin. This could be the news we've been waiting for. Try to remain calm."

He fell back into his chair. "I want to be there. Where is it?"

"I'm not prepared to divulge that information just yet, Martin. We won't let you down. If Adele is there, we'll find her and have the three of you reunited ASAP, I promise."

Just then, the waitress arrived with their food. The inspector stepped away from the table and sat in one of the sofas on the other side of the room where she continued to make calls. Martin kept one eye on her as he tucked into his bacon sandwich and chips. His appetite had wavered and he picked at his lunch, while Debs tucked into hers without a problem.

He noticed the inspector shaking her head a lot and that her fist was clenched beside her, beating the chair. *That doesn't look good! Please, please let Adele be safe.*

Eventually, once their lunch plates had been whisked away, the inspector approached them again with an update. "I'm sorry, it wasn't good news. The child at the property turned out to be a little boy with shoulder-length hair."

Debs broke down and Martin immediately comforted her. "I thought it was her. How many more times are we going to have to go through similar experiences? Getting our hopes up only for them to be dashed?" Debs mumbled.

"If you'd rather I don't tell you in the future, I'm okay with that," Cobbs replied.

"No. I want to know, every step of the way, I want to know what's going on with the investigation," Debs confirmed.

"That's what I thought. Okay, this time was a negative result, but hopefully, it won't be long before we have a positive one for you. Again, I apologise if you felt I built your hopes up. I think it's a lesson for us all to not take things for granted until there is some degree of certainty attached to the news."

"I agree," Martin replied. "Are you all right, Debs?" Up until now, she had been the stronger one, and it was hard for him to see the tough shell encasing her disintegrate before his eyes.

"I will be. It's my own fault. I've told myself to remain calm. I've been practising my yoga techniques and what I've learnt from my instructor about keeping calm, and up until now, it's worked. Hearing that she might have been found broke something inside and the dam burst when it turned out to be a mistake. I'll gather my thoughts together and stop being a blubbering wreck."

He held her hand. "You're allowed to show your feelings, no one will think any worse of you, Debs."

"Martin is right, Deborah. I'm sorry to have given you false hope only to strip it away again within minutes. I feel bad about that," the inspector said.

"No, no. Please, don't feel bad. We want to know these things, don't we, Martin?"

"Yes, she's right. I think being in the dark will only prove to be more damaging in the long run."

"As you wish. I'm going to get the teams together now. See what their reaction is to calling it a day out here, if that's okay with you?"

"If you think that's the right call, then Debs and I won't stand in your way."

As soon as the inspector left the room Martin gathered Debs in his arms and the dam burst again. He mopped up her tears and rocked her back and forth for the next ten minutes, until she lifted her head and kissed him on the cheek.

"I'm fine now. My old nan used to swear by a good cry, now and again. It's good for the system, apparently."

Grinning, he said, "Maybe I should try it sometimes."

"What now?"

Martin glanced out of the window and saw the dejected crowd dispersing. "I suppose we should head back to Liverpool; as much as that thought horrifies me, I think we have to take what the inspector said on board and believe that someone, an opportunist, took Adele. I detest the thought of her being with someone else. Furthermore, if ever I lay my hands on the bastard who grabbed her, I'm going to bloody tear him to shreds, limb by limb. I'll search the internet for the most gruesome ways to kill people and hold him captive until he cries for mercy and then I'll up the ante."

Shocked, Debs asked, "You're serious, aren't you?"

"You bet I am. What gives a person the right to take someone else's child? They're in the wrong, *not* me."

"My nan had another saying she used to band about too."

He tilted his head and asked, "Which was?"

"Two wrongs don't make a right."

"Ah, that old chestnut. Maybe she's right, but you know what? I couldn't give a toss, at the end of the day, torturing the culprit will make me feel good inside. At the moment, I'm raw with guilt and helplessness."

"You have nothing to feel guilty about, but I hear you on the helplessness. I suppose it goes with the territory. Talking about driving home, when we get there, what will you do? Go back to Louise's?"

"No. There's no future for us, not now. I'll stay at a friend's house. I'm sure Sean and Tania will put me up for a few days."

"Or…"

"Or?" He gripped her hand.

"You could move back into the family home again. After all, you're still paying half the mortgage and towards some of the bills, or had you forgotten that?"

"Blimey, is that truly an option? After the way I treated you?"

"Let's just say, my heart is ruling my head on this one."

"You're such a wonderfully forgiving person, Debs. I'm not worthy to know you, let alone anything else…" He let his words die off, not wishing to ruin anything.

"Nonsense. We all make mistakes in this life, Martin. Let's move on within reason, and deal with whatever lies in our future together. We'll be far stronger as a unit than if we dealt with this shit separately."

"You took the words out of my mouth." He leaned over and kissed her on the lips; a kiss that was neither fleeting nor lingering, it settled somewhere in between, which seemed to suit both of them.

. . .

*T*he inspector returned to see them half an hour later, to give them an update. They had a coffee together. She laid her cards on the table, and she was honest and forthright in what she told them. "I would advise you to go home today. I can honestly say I can't see any point in you remaining in the area. However, I also want to assure you that we will continue the search for Adele, maybe not physically out here, because I believe it will be a waste of time, but we'll search every means available to us, continue to work with the nearby forces in the hope that some clues or evidence will surface that urge us to investigate. You have my number, don't hesitate to call me if you're unsure about anything you hear in the news. I will warn you though, some journalists are in the job to make mischief and to further their careers, just be aware of that whilst watching the news and reading the newspapers."

"We will. Can we ask that you give us regular updates?" Martin suggested.

"Of course, every other day?"

"That would be great. We'll give you our mobile numbers."

"I know this probably looks to you like we're giving up, but I promise you, our investigation has only just begun. I also want to warn you that there are sure to be numerous dark days ahead of you. I'm glad you have each other to lean on, that will be a bonus for you in the battle that lies ahead."

Debs and Martin clung to each other's hands. "We're going to help each other get through this. Reunited for however long it takes to find Adele. Who knows what will happen after she comes home?" Debs said, smiling at Martin.

"I'm glad. There's nothing worse than warring parents who have separated and are intent on blaming each other when things get bad. It helps no one and risks putting the child in further jeopardy, in my opinion."

"Exactly. We want to thank you for keeping us up to date, Inspector. For treating us like human beings and not casting our concerns aside," Martin said.

"Different officers deal with victims' families in varying ways. I've always found the direct approach to be the fairest and most productive to all concerned. I'll be in touch soon. Have a safe trip home."

"Thank you. We're glad to have you leading the investigation," Martin replied, offering his hand to shake. The inspector smiled and shook it.

"Teamwork, all round, remember that." She left the room and they watched her go in silence until the door shut.

"At least I don't have the feeling we're all alone," Debs said.

Martin watched the inspector issue instructions to her team outside. "I agree."

8

During the journey back south, Debs had insisted Martin should drive. The car remained quiet most of the time. Not an awkward silence, but a comfortable one. Each of them lost, deep in their own thoughts. Martin found himself keeping vigilant throughout. As he passed every car, he couldn't help but cast a cursory glance at the passengers. Ever hopeful that Adele might be staring back at him. It was a daft thought; nevertheless, it was one that made the journey more bearable at times.

"Do you have the rest of the week off?" Debs asked when they were about twenty miles from home.

"Yes, I'd booked the cottage for a week. Are you supposed to be at work?"

"No, I booked the week off to put my feet up and make the most of Adele not being around." Her voice became strained.

He reached for her hand. "I know what you meant. Don't get upset, love. We'll get through this. She'll come back to us soon, I'm sure she will."

"I hope you're right. I'm trying to keep upbeat about it, but every now and then, a simple thought catches me out."

"It's the same for me. I know you said to stop thinking about it and blaming myself, but it's easier said than done. The what-ifs coursing through my mind are driving me nuts."

"Remember what I said, you need to let the guilt go; otherwise, it's going to make you ill. Then where would I be, without you around to comfort me during my darkest days?"

He brought her hand up to his mouth and kissed it gently. "I'm not going anywhere, I promise."

"Good. We're more powerful as a team. What will you do about your belongings?"

"Ugh, I'll need to drop over and have a chat with Louise soon. It's only fair to let her know what's been decided. If you're still okay about me moving back in with you?"

"Of course. I'd be lost without you beside me. And that's not me being slushy, it's a fact. Let's face it, neither of us knows what lies ahead of us. I sense a rollercoaster ride of emotions could overwhelm us. Having you around will make it easier to deal with. I'm grateful to you moving back in, I know the decision wasn't an easy one for you to make, love."

"I'm determined to make things work between us, Debs. I can never expect you to fully forgive me, but I want to assure you that I will never stray in the future. If this awful incident has taught me anything, it's that we belong together."

Debs kissed his hand in return. "I agree. The past is the past, some things are best left there. Can I ask you something personal?"

"Oh, God, here goes. What's that?"

"Why did Louise's husband walk out on her and the kids?"

"I asked the same question and never really received a proper answer. She told me that one day he walked out and never came back."

"What? Don't you think that's weird?"

"Yes, definitely. I did ask the question, but she couldn't supply any answers. I asked if they were happy up until that point, and she replied, yes, as far as she knew. I suppose it goes to prove you really don't know what's going on in someone's head until it's too late."

"That's terrible, abandoning the kids like that. And they've had no contact with him at all?"

"Nope, nothing."

"I hate to say it, but could he have committed suicide? Was that ever a consideration?"

Martin nodded and indicated to pass another car on his left. He peeked through the window as he sped past. "It was considered, but discounted pretty quickly by Louise and Chris's parents."

"I see. What about his job? Don't tell me he left that as well?"

"First place Louise checked. He'd handed his notice in two weeks before. Even pretended to Louise that he was going to work the week before he took off."

"Wow, so it was... what do the police call it? Pre-something."

"Premeditated, yep, so it would seem. Louise even tried to employ a private detective to do some digging for her, but he drew a blank as well."

"Bloody hell. I suppose if someone chooses to just disappear like that, there's very little anyone else can do about it. I feel sorry for Louise, now she's about to lose you as well."

"I know. I feel like shit for walking away, but I wouldn't be able to keep up the pretence, Debs. I don't love her, I'm still in love with you."

Debs swallowed and sniffled. He handed her a tissue from the central console. "All we need now is to get our baby back and then we can be a proper family again."

"It'll happen. Fingers crossed it's soon."

Once they pulled up outside what was to become Martin's home again, he unloaded the car while Debs entered the house to put the kettle on. He looked up and down the street and caught a few curtains twitching here and there. He shrugged and carried his case inside.

They sat down in the newly fitted kitchen, something they'd put in a month or two before he'd walked out, with a loan he was still paying off, and switched on the TV. They watched the afternoon bulletin together. Seeing their beautiful Adele's face on the screen, Debs' head dipped and her shoulders shook. He gathered her in his arms, putting aside his own helpless emotions to take care of Debs.

"It's hard, I know. But the more they keep showing her photo, the more likely it is we'll get her back, sweetheart."

"I know. Oh, God, I miss her so much. I've tried to be strong, to keep my emotions in check, but it's proving harder every hour she's missing. Maybe coming back here has made it worse, I don't know. I feel her all around me. I'm aware her toys are stored away in the cupboard over there. I wish she was here making a bloody mess. I swear, if she comes back, I will never curse her again for leaving her toys lying around for me to stub my toe on."

"*When* she comes back, not if. I suppose every parent in our situation has the same conversation with their family members. It's a tough position to find ourselves in. We'll get through it. Think of the happy times you spent with her. The holidays we went on. Remember that time we went on a mini-break to Guernsey? She loved it there, messing about on the beach, chasing the seagulls as they landed, scavenging for the odd scraps of food the holidaymakers had left behind."

"I do remember. She was three at the time. She's been driving us crazy ever since to go back there."

"I wish I'd taken her to the beach the other day, instead of the lake. It was a toss-up between the two. If only I had, we wouldn't be sitting here, struggling to get a hold of our feelings."

The doorbell rang to interrupt him. He cleared the lump in his throat and went to open the door, then paused at the doorway. "God, I forgot myself then. It should be you answering the door, Debs."

She waved the suggestion away. "No, it shouldn't, please, I'd rather you do it."

He smiled and then walked into the hallway to answer it. Standing on the doorstep was a young man in a suit. "Yes?"

"Mr Jenkins, I'm Todd Wilkins from the Liverpool Echo. I was wondering if you had time for a quick chat."

"About what?" Martin responded, acting dumb.

"Come now, sir, there's no need for you to be so coy; we both know why I'm here, interested in speaking with you."

"Yeah, we do. Look, we'd rather be left alone right now. We appreciate what you're all doing for us, keeping our daughter in the minds of the general public, but I held a press conference up in The Lakes, that took a lot out of me, as you can imagine. We don't want to be bothered every five minutes with a journalist from a different newspaper, knocking at our door. I'm sure you can understand our feelings on that issue."

"I can. Look, I'm experienced in these types of cases. Not bragging or anything, but in the past, when a child has gone missing and the parents have opened up to me and the readers, it has had startling results."

"Meaning what?"

"That the child has been found and returned home."

"In every case?"

"More or less." Wilkins grinned.

Martin shook his head. "I'm sorry, I repeat, as much as we welcome you guys sharing our daughter's disappearance, I don't feel comfortable opening up to the press every five minutes. We're quite private people and this kind of intrusion is only going to make our emotional ride a darn sight worse."

"Are you two back together?"

Wilkins' question rocked him. Martin frowned. "What does that have to do with you?"

The journalist shrugged and smirked. "I think you are, which again, in itself could make a wonderful headline for the paper."

Anger surged. "That's enough. Goodbye, Mr Wilkins." The door slammed in the reporter's surprised face.

"Who was at the door?" Debs asked the moment he stepped back into the kitchen.

"A bloody nosey reporter. Wanting another sodding exclusive with his paper."

Debs held her head in her hands. "Is that what our life is going to consist of in the days ahead of us? Us dodging the cameras and reporters? If it is, I'm not sure I'm going to be able to cope."

"It won't, I promise. Why don't I make us another cup of coffee? That usually makes the world feel a better place again, doesn't it?"

"Okay. I suppose I should think about getting something organised for dinner as well."

"Burger and chips from the takeaway around the corner will do for me, don't feel like you have to cook for us, sweetheart."

"Phew! That's a relief, not sure I'm up to much. It's been a hectic twenty-four hours or so, you know how much I hate travelling."

"Why don't you take your drink upstairs and have a lie-down?"

"Would you mind? What will you do?"

"Don't worry about me, I'm sure I'll find something to occupy my mind. I might even call around to Louise's and pick up the rest of my stuff, if that's all right? If you're a hundred percent sure about me moving back in here with you."

Debs hopped off her stool, stood in front of him and slid her arms around his neck. "Of course I am. There are no doubts running through my mind, I can assure you. I need you and your support, Martin, like I've never needed it before."

"You've got it." He kissed her deeply and then groaned. "I think we better stop before we *both* end up in bed."

She smirked. "Fine by me."

He kissed the tip of her nose. "Go, I'll bring your coffee up when it's made."

Debs trotted out of the room and he proceeded to get a coffee ready, just for her. The kettle boiled, and he took her drink upstairs.

A strange feeling descended as he walked up the stairs. It had been a while since he'd ventured into the bedroom with Debs, and he wasn't sure how he'd react once he walked in. Before he reached the master bedroom, though, he had to pass Adele's room. The door was ajar. With one finger, he poked at it and the door slowly swung open to reveal his daughter's pink princess bed, the one he'd put together himself three years earlier when she'd grown out of her cot. His heartstrings tugged as he took in all her cuddly toys and the dolls lined up on the floor along the skirting board, similar to the way he'd found Lucy Lou back at the cottage. Maybe Adele had placed the doll in that position under the bed, after all.

He crept into the room as if a magnet was drawing him in. Once inside, he turned slowly, taking in all her possessions; then he closed his eyes and imagined her back there, in her room, snuggled beneath the bright pink quilt cover, smiling up at him. When he opened his eyes again, the reality hit him like a sledgehammer to the gut. Martin placed the mug of coffee on the small bedside table, sat on the edge of the bed and broke down.

Debs must have heard his heart rending sobs because she appeared in the doorway seconds later. "Oh, darling, you shouldn't have come in here. It's why I went straight to my bedroom. I knew the devastation it would cause if I opened the door and poked my head in."

"I miss her so much. My God, I need her to come home. She's only just come back to me after all these months apart and I failed her. I let her out of my sight and someone bloody took her. You can't imagine the guilt I feel knowing all this could have been avoided. If only I'd put Adele's needs first… we wouldn't be in this position and she would be with us now."

"No, you're wrong. First of all, you're not to blame. Secondly, if Adele hadn't gone missing, then we wouldn't have been thrown back together."

Rubbing a hand across his face, he smiled at her. "I know. Let's hope it's an omen and she comes back to us soon. I'm sorry for breaking down, I'm trying my best to remain strong for both of us. It's hard though."

"I know you are. Hey, you're emotionally overwrought, go get your stuff and I'll knock us up a nice meal to celebrate your coming home. Forget the takeaway, I want to show willing and look after my man instead."

"No, I refuse to let you do that, you need your rest, love. I'll pick up a takeaway on the way home, and you can cook us a special meal tomorrow, how does that sound?"

"Okay, sounds good to me."

They shared another kiss and left the room. Debs slipped into bed and he put the mug down beside her. "I won't be long. Is there anything else you need?"

"Only you. I love you, Martin. I've never stopped loving you."

He felt elated and her heaven-sent words plugged a gaping hole in his heart. "I know. I feel exactly the same. I can't tell you how sorry I am for leaving you. Again, if I hadn't left, Adele would still be with us now."

Debs smiled and shook her head. "You mustn't keep punishing yourself like that. We can't turn back the clock, neither of us can."

"I know. Let's not get maudlin, I want to try and remain upbeat about her coming back to us. The alternative is for us to mope around and that's not going to get us anywhere, is it?"

"You're wise to think that way. I'll be fine, leave me and go. I'll drink my coffee and then snuggle down for a snooze."

Debs' eyelids fluttered as she struggled to keep awake. "I won't be long. I'm not going to get into an argument with her; if she starts, I'll leave my stuff there and come home straight away. So you may see me sooner than you think."

"I hope she doesn't kick off. See you later."

He bent to kiss her, and she hugged him tightly and smiled.

*M*artin sucked in a deep breath and left the car. He had parked in front of his own vehicle, the one Louise had driven back from The Lakes. He'd need to make arrangements to pick that up another time, when Debs was feeling up to it. He rattled his key in his trouser pocket, but chose to ring the bell instead.

Louise seemed confused when she opened the door to him. "Oh, hi, why didn't you use your key?"

"I forgot I had it," he lied. Then admitted, "It didn't feel right, sorry."

Louise stood back and motioned for him to come in. Cautiously, he stepped into the hallway of the Victorian house he'd come to regard as his home for the past eight or nine months.

"Any news?" Louise asked. She led the way through the regency-coloured hallway to the kitchen at the rear.

"Nothing so far. We drove back this afternoon. I settled Debs at the house and decided to come over and see you."

"That was kind of you."

He detected a note of sarcasm in her tone. "Sorry I haven't called you. I've been up to my neck in the search, speaking to the media and the police. Time passes by so quickly when you're being bombarded from all angles."

"I can imagine. Had I been in your position, though, I would have kept you updated. I suppose that's the difference between us."

"Don't start, Louise." He went on the defensive.

She leaned against the quartz worktop and crossed her arms. "Don't start? I make a simple comment and that's the first words out of your mouth?"

"We hardly parted on speaking terms, did we?"

"And whose fault was that? I left you a note at the cottage and I told you to your face, several times how sorry I am. No matter how many times I say it, it's never going to be enough, is it? Go on, tell me, truthfully."

He wandered over to the bi-fold doors and stared out at the garden which was full of equipment for the kids, her kids. And again, his heart sank. "No."

She came to stand beside him and tugged on his arm, forcing him to face her and have the conversation he was reluctant to have now that he was here.

"No? What are you saying, Martin?"

He turned to her and watched the colour instantly drain from her face. "That it's over between us."

"Jesus! Why? Because of one lousy mistake?"

He gritted his teeth and then let out a harsh laugh. "In my book, it was a pretty *massive* mistake."

"For which I apologised. I'll feel guilty about not keeping a closer eye on Adele, *your* child, for the rest of my bloody life. It's not like I did it intentionally... wait, you can't possibly think that?"

He shrugged.

Louise let out a screech and slapped him, hard. So hard his head snapped to the side and rebounded. He narrowed his eyes and glared at her. "You heartless fucking prick. How dare you come here and accuse me of intentionally taking my eye off the ball, allowing your daughter to wander off like that?"

"She didn't."

Her brow furrowed. "What? I don't understand."

"The inspector in charge of the case suspects Adele was abducted. Haven't you seen the news?"

"No. I've kept the TV and radio off since we got back; all this has been too traumatic for Matilda and Jake, so I made sure they didn't have access to any of the news reports. That's by the by, what makes the inspector think she has been abducted?"

"Protecting your kids, as any mother should." He grumbled. "The scent for the sniffer dogs went cold at the road. They believe someone probably led her away and drove off."

"Oh fuck. I never imagined anything along those lines might have taken place. No wonder you're angry with me."

"Angry is one word for it. I can never forgive you, Louise, as harsh as that sounds, even to my ears. I would be letting my daughter down if I did."

She stumbled backwards and clutched at the dining room chair behind her. "It needn't be over between us, we could mend things, couldn't we?"

"What? I find it incredible that you could possibly think things could ever be right between us." He shook his head and let out a guttural groan. "You thought we could get past this and carry on with 'our happy little family' vibe? There's no way I could do that, not now." His words came out more cruelly than he'd intended. The whole conversation hadn't gone the way he'd imagined. She pushed his buttons, thinking they could continue being the ideal couple.

Louise sank into the chair and slapped a hand to her cheek. "My God, you're serious, aren't you? You're intent on blaming me for this... God, I never thought I'd hear those words come out of your mouth. It was an *accident*, a misguided lapse in concentration. Actually, it wasn't. Yes, I'm guilty of putting my own daughter first, because at the time, it was Matilda who needed me. If that's me being a bad parent, then yes, heap it on me. But you're wrong. This isn't about who needed my attention more on the day. You only had one child, an older child to look after, I had two, one aged six and Adele who is five, no mean feat to contend with, I'm sure you'll agree. At least any normal, fair-minded person would come down on my side. Why can't you see that?"

It was as if she'd practised her speech a dozen times over before their meeting, but no matter how she tried to paint what happened that day, he was having none of it. "You've got your take on it and I have mine. It doesn't matter who comes down on the side of being right or wrong, the conclusion will always be the same. Adele, my five-year-old daughter is missing."

She stared at him and shook her head. "I can't take it. The thought of you heaping the blame on me." Tears emerged, and she angrily swiped them away. "How can you stand there and speak to me like this, after all we've been through together?"

"Don't be such a drama queen. We've been together eight months after we started a damn illicit relationship at work. It was hardly the love affair of the century, was it?"

Her hand reached out and grabbed the salt pot. She aimed it at him and it hit him in the arm, stunning both of them. "I'm sorry, I didn't mean to do that."

"If that's what our relationship has come down to, then it's a good job I'm leaving."

"No. Don't say that! You can't go. I won't let you."

He leaned in and sneered, "You haven't got a choice."

He opened the bottom drawer on his immediate right and tore off a black sack, then marched through the house and up the stairs to the bedroom they used to share. Thankfully, Louise didn't bother following him. He'd had enough arguments to fill a lifetime over the past few days. Functioning on the emotions rising and falling within him, he removed all his clothes from the wardrobe and thrust them into the black bag, not concerned whether they ended up creased or not. He did the same with his underwear and T-shirts from the one drawer Louise had kindly given up when he'd moved in. He wasn't really one for shoes, so there was nothing to pack there as they were all back at Debs' house in the suitcase he'd taken on holiday.

Footsteps sounded on the stairs, and Louise appeared in the doorway, her arms folded as she leaned against the doorframe. "You're a cruel man, Martin Jenkins. One day in the future, when Adele finds her way back home, I hope you recall what was said here today and the disgusting way you've treated me."

"If she ever comes home, no doubt you're right. I won't apologise for telling the truth, Louise. Most men would have resorted to name-calling by now, but I haven't sunk to that level. My daughter means the world to me, I've fought the system for months to spend time with her; and when I do, she vanishes. Have you even considered how the fuck that is going to look when the judge finds out?"

"My God, that thought is at the forefront of your mind? Is that why you're moving out, probably back in with her?"

"No, it's not. Don't even think that way. During our time together, I've realised I still love Debs; I don't think I ever fell out of love with her, if I'm honest. Our time together has been a mistake, one that I'll regret for the rest of my life."

Louise ran at him, and she thumped both hands on his chest, sending him stumbling backwards into the wardrobe. "You bastard. How can you say that? I opened my heart and my home to you. You used me because Deborah kicked you out and you had nowhere else to go, go on, admit it."

"I didn't. I can't even remember how all this came about. My life was in a spin back then, nothing by comparison to what it is now. I'm sorry things didn't work out between us. But I can't apologise for blaming you, not yet, not until I have my little girl back. If that makes me a vile person, well then, so be it. I have to go now, Debs needs me."

He walked towards the door and felt a thud on his back. Glancing down at his feet, he saw the ornate silver brush Louise had inherited from her grandmother. "Really? Do you feel better now, Louise?"

"No. I feel like shit. All this has had a detrimental effect on me, Martin, whether you want to believe it or not. I'm gutted about Adele. I'm not in the habit of repeating myself, nor should I when you down-right refuse to bloody listen to me. As a mother, this is eating me up inside. At a time when I need your support, you're turning your damn back on me, only making things ten times worse."

He stood anchored to the spot as her words sank in; for the first time, he could see deep into her soul and had mixed feelings running through him. Was he right to blame her? *Of course I am. Maybe I'm guilty of being too damning, though. As a mother, she should realise what the loss of a child means to a parent.* Unable to find the words he needed to put the situation right, he turned and walked down the stairs.

"You utter fucking bastard! You may never forgive me, Martin, but equally, I will never forgive you for making me feel the way I do. I hope for Christ's sake Adele comes home because if she doesn't, I know this is going to eat away at you and your hatred for me will grow each and every day she's missing. To have someone share your bed with you one day, only for them to turn their back on you the next, is soul-destroying and totally overwhelming. Go, Martin, I hope you take a long hard look at the way you've spoken to me today."

"Goodbye, Louise. I'll pick up the car another day."

With that, he left the house. She screamed his name, but he didn't bother going back inside.

She was dead to him now.

9

Why is this damn road blocked? Martin tried to squeeze past a few cars that were jutting out awkwardly when he returned to Debs' house. It wasn't until he looked beyond them, at what might be causing the hold-up, that he spotted the huge crowd outside the house. He abandoned the car where it was and ran the length of the road as fast as any sprinter could, if the burning in his lungs was anything to go by.

"What are you doing here? Get back. How dare you? I'm going to call the police if you don't get out of here. Fucking let me through! Get out of my way." The more he pushed, the more the crowd closed ranks and refused to let him pass. In the end, he carried out his threat and called the police.

During the agonising wait, the crowd badgered him with questions. *Bloody journalists!*

His gaze was drawn to the man at the front of the crowd, leaning against the door to the house. Todd Wilkins. *Bloody bastard! He's rallied the damn troops, all because I wouldn't do an exclusive with him. Is this what we're going to have to contend with going forward? Jesus, I hope Debs is okay. I need to get in there and see if she's all right. Her nerves were frayed before, they're going to be a darn sight worse now.*

"Mr Jenkins, any word about Adele yet? How are you and your wife holding up? Weren't you separated? Are you back together now? Do you know what has happened to your daughter? Are you satisfied with how the investigation is going or are you frustrated they haven't found her yet? Have they found her? Do they know where she is? Did she walk off? Get abducted? Has the kidnapper called you asking for a ransom to be paid? What about Deborah, how is she holding up? What about you, how are you doing? What have the police told you about the investigation? How is it going? Are they any closer to getting your daughter back? What happened? Why was she left alone at the time of her disappearance?

Questions, questions, all mind-numbing. Some I just can't answer and others I have no intention of answering. How dare they be here, pestering us when we're at our lowest ebb? Vultures, picking over the bones of a situation just to get a story. Bastards, the lot of them.

Finally, a patrol car showed up around ten minutes later. It was the longest ten minutes of his life, apart from the day Adele went missing.

"All right, all right. Let the gentleman pass. What's all this about?" the older officer said, pulling at some of the journalists.

"We're entitled to be here, we're trying to help the family," one of the female journalists insisted.

One of the two uniformed officers got in her face and shouted, "You think harassing the poor family like this is helping them? How do you figure that one out?"

The woman's mouth opened and shut a few times, imitating a fish gasping for breath out of water. She took a step back when she drew a blank to his question. The officer then proceeded to tear his way through the crowd while his colleague nudged Martin ahead of him and brought up the rear. He was in a police sandwich being escorted to the door and the crowd were being eased back, their futile questions ignored.

Eventually, they reached the front door, and Martin came face to face with Todd Wilkins. "You, I hope you die a long and painful death for putting me and my family through this."

Todd smirked, seemingly unimpressed by Martin's outburst. "What have I done? The public have a right to know what's going on."

"Why hound us? As if we bloody know, we're not in charge of the ruddy investigation, are we? Go pester another unfortunate soul, desperate for help, because I told you earlier, we've said all we're going to say to the press. We're grateful for you trying to help us, but not like this."

"You'll change your mind, people in your situation always do, come the end."

"You're going to have a bloody long wait. We won't be changing our minds. Now do one."

Todd folded his arms and shook his head.

The officers urged Martin to go inside the house, but when he slipped the key into the lock and opened the door, the chain barred him. "Sweetheart, it's me. Can you open the door?"

"No. Not until those horrible people go away," Debs screeched. It sounded like she was on the other side of the door in the hallway, but he really couldn't tell.

Martin glanced at the officers. "She's refusing to open up until these people go. Can't you force them to leave?"

One of the officers shook his head. "We've done as much as we can, unless they start to make a nuisance of themselves."

"What? And you don't regard blocking the road and camping out on my doorstep being a nuisance? God, give me bloody strength. I need to get in there, Debs needs me. Don't you think she's going through enough at the moment? Why do we have to contend with this shit when we're already suffering the loss of our child?"

"We're doing our best, sir. We'll remain here for the time being, until the fuss dies down. They'll soon get bored if you ignore them."

"You reckon?" he asked sarcastically, noting the twinkle in Wilkins' eyes. He turned back to the door and spoke quietly to Debs through the gap. "Honey, please, just open the door and let me in. I can't help you if you shut me out like this. Please, let me in."

The chain jingled on the other side and the door eased open. Martin issued a quick thank you to the officers and slipped through the gap. He slammed the door behind him and gathered the distraught Debs in his arms. "My God, how long have they been here?"

"They arrived not five minutes after you left. It's been terrible, horrendous. They've been knocking on the doors and windows, demanding to speak to me. Why? Why do that? We don't know anything. They should be hounding the police for answers instead of badgering us for any news." She placed her head on his chest, and the sobs soon followed.

"Come on, let's get you settled in the lounge."

She stared at him, petrified. "No, they'll be able to see us."

"They won't, I'll pull the curtains across, block them out. Come on, Debs, do it for me."

She finally agreed, but held back until Martin had used the curtains to shut out the rest of the world and told her the coast was clear. Debs sat on the edge of the sofa, her hands clenched tightly together until her knuckles turned white.

"Can I get you a coffee or something stronger, perhaps?"

"Maybe a tot of brandy will help calm my nerves. I didn't think you were coming back; I was so scared, of them, of you not returning. I couldn't handle it if you left me, Martin, not again."

He sat next to her and enfolded her in his arms. "I'm not going anywhere, love. I promise you."

"But I thought you were going to pick up your stuff and yet you've come back empty-handed."

"I haven't. My bag is in the car, I couldn't get any closer. It's parked up the road. Hey, you can't get rid of me so easily." He kissed her on the cheek.

"I'm glad. I couldn't handle this on my own. I don't know where to turn for help. We haven't heard anything from the police. I fear I'm going to end up losing my mind at this rate."

"Nonsense. You said it yourself, we're stronger together, as a team. I'm not about to up sticks and leave you again, sweetheart. You're going to have to believe me when I tell you that. I'll fix us a couple of drinks. Damn, I forgot to stop off and pick up a takeaway on the way home. It was as if something was urging me to get back here straight away."

"It doesn't matter. I don't think I could eat anything, anyway."

"You have to eat to keep your strength up. I'll fix us some nibbles to go with our drink, how's that?"

"Okay."

He left her and walked into the kitchen. Luckily, there was no way the journalists could get into the back garden—it was walled with a small solid gate at the end which Debs always ensured was bolted and never used. Saying that, there was nothing to stop the more determined journalists from climbing the wall. He shook his head, shaking loose the image. He was halfway through preparing the plateful of cheese and biscuits when his mobile rang. He answered it with an abrupt tone, "Hello?"

Nothing.

He listened more intently and could just make out someone breathing.

"Who is this?" he demanded, his heart rate notching up a little.

Still no response.

"If you don't tell me who this is I'm going to ring the police, they'll track you down, they have ways of tracing incoming calls. Now who the hell is this?"

"Martin, it's me. Your mother."

"Jesus, Mum, you had me bloody worried there for a minute. Why do that to me, knowing we're obviously going out of our minds here?"

"I apologise. I didn't think. Please, don't be angry with me. I'm trying to make amends."

"For what? Months of ignoring me? Why the sudden change of heart after all this time? Guilt, is that it? Your guilty conscience pricking you into action now that your granddaughter has gone missing?"

"Don't say it like that. Maybe it's a bit of the truth, but I miss speaking with you. Visiting you. Please, I want Adele back as much as you do, don't shut me out, not now," his mother said meekly and with a certain degree of hesitancy.

He closed his eyes, pictured his mother's ageing face and shuddered. She'd had months to ring him and yet she'd chosen to cut him out of her life completely; and now, here she was, expecting to be welcomed back with open arms. "To be honest with you, Debs and I are on the edge at the moment. I can't think about anything or anyone else, other than Adele. I don't have it in me to tiptoe around others in case I step on their fragile feelings or say the wrong thing."

"I hear you. I'm sorry, the last thing I want to be is a nuisance at such a troubling time. I just needed to hear your voice and to tell you that I'm here for you if you need me."

"Thanks. I'm not sure what else you want me to say other than that, Mum. If you want to get back into my life, then it's going to take time to mend things. I haven't got it in me to forgive and forget at the moment. I'm sure you'll be able to understand that, given the circumstances."

"I do. I'm prepared to wait," she stated, her voice trembling with emotion. "But please, before you put the phone down on me again, I want you to know that you've never been far from my mind. I've thought about you daily, as any mother would. I just haven't had the courage to phone you to put things back on course between us."

"That's fine. Leave it with me, Mum. I need to go and get back to Debs now. We've got a hoard of bloody press outside. I reckon they're going to camp out on the doorstep for days. It's tough to handle, as I'm sure you can appreciate. Debs needs me by her side."

"I'm glad you're back together. I never thought you should have left her and gone off with that floozy in the first place."

He groaned and rolled his eyes. "See, now saying things like that is only going to drive another wedge between us, is that what you want?"

"Oh no, please, don't say that. I didn't mean it. Me and my big mouth. I'm so sorry. Forgive me, no, don't hang up on me. I couldn't bear it if you hung up."

"I'm going, Mother. I'm lacking the mental prowess to deal with your shenanigans at present. I'll be in touch soon."

"Martin, no… please, Martin. Don't hang—"

He cut her off. His mind whirled as he finished preparing their snack, not that he was in the mood to eat now, after speaking with his mother. The trouble with Kathlyn was, that she was a desperately needy person, always had been and always would be. Up until his father's death, he'd been able to cope with her mood swings, but once his father was laid to rest, that's when the neediness had shown its true colours. Even though she ran a successful hairdressing business, which employed ten stylists, her home life had been a stark contrast.

No, he couldn't handle her suffocating him, not at this time, not when Adele was out there somewhere, crying out for his help. His primary consideration remained with his child and it always would. Harsh as it might sound, his mother had lived her life; his little girl was just starting out on her incredible journey. Emotion reared its head, anger being the most prominent of all. He threw the sharp knife into the kitchen sink and spread his arms on the worktop as if trying to gain strength from the granite surface. He needed something to ease the anger and tension attacking his insides and causing his muscles to seize up.

After giving himself a kick up the backside, he completed his task and carried the tray into the lounge. Debs was staring at the TV screen. On it was his daughter's beautiful smiling face, with the prominent scar on her right cheekbone where she'd fallen off her bike a couple of years before and the wound needed stitches at the hospital. What a day that had been, burdened with anguish. Adele had been inconsolable, fearful of the nurses and the doctor as they tried to approach her with the needle. She'd screamed and needed to be sedated in the end so the doctor could carry out the procedure. It had taken three stitches to stem the bleeding and to pull the skin together. Over time, as the doctor had assured them, the wound healed, but he'd told them there would always be a slight imperfection. He'd laughed and called it a war wound. Martin had also laughed until Debs had struck him, admonishing him for treating their daughter's discomfort lightly.

He placed the tray on the coffee table and sat beside Debs who appeared to be mesmerised by the image. Once the newsreader moved on to the next story, Debs just sat there, staring at the screen, tears rolling down her ashen face. "Are you all right, Debs?"

"I'll never be all right again, not until she comes back to us. How could anyone take her, knowing she's only five and desperate to be with her mummy? That's what I can't get my head around."

"And her daddy." He felt the need to correct her.

"Of course. I'm sorry. I'm talking gibberish, you knew what I meant."

"I did. Why don't I put on a film instead of watching every news bulletin that comes around during the day?"

"I wouldn't be able to concentrate. I need to see her, to know that they're showing her face all the time. Oh, Martin, what will happen to her, to us, if the person who took her refuses to give her up?"

"I'll never stop asking myself the same question, love. We need to keep optimistic that someone will see her soon and report the sighting to the police."

"Have you spoken to them yet?"

"I was going to call the inspector later on today." He glanced at the clock above the fireplace and sighed. "I didn't realise it was so late."

"It's only six-thirty, please, give her a call."

He took a sip of the brandy and dialled the number. The inspector answered the call on the second ring.

"Hello, DI Cobbs."

"Hello, Inspector. It's Martin Jenkins. Just wanted to let you know we're back safely and ask if there had been any further developments since our departure."

"Ah, it's good to hear from you, Martin. Sorry, no, nothing to report as yet. I want to assure you, my team are putting in the extra hours on this one, but sadly, nothing has come to light yet. We're not going to give up, though, you have my word."

"Thank you. Will you call us if anything surfaces?"

"Of course. How's Deborah?"

"We're both a mess. We've got dozens of damn journalists camped out on our doorstep. The police had to escort me to my front door when I went out earlier."

"Damn, I'm so sorry to hear that. Keep onto the local police if it continues, they can move them on if they become a nuisance. You're going to have to ride the storm. Once these guys pick up on a scent like this, well, sometimes they don't know when to back off. Stay strong."

"Thanks. I hate to ask, but is there any way you can get in touch with the local police for us? Apprise them of the situation?"

"I've already spoken to a DI Lance Cooper. He told me he'd leave it a day or two and then visit you to lend his support. Do you want me to get in touch with him, ask him to come and see you ASAP?"

"Yes, if you wouldn't mind. Thank you for thinking of us."

"Of course. Any problems, be sure to ring me. I'll do the same the second we hear any good news, I promise."

"Thank you. We'll do that. Goodbye, Inspector."

"Take care of each other."

"We will." Martin ended the call and dropped his mobile onto the table.

Debs' shoulders trembled and the emotion she'd been suppressing broke free. "I can't cope with this, Martin. Why are they doing this to us? We're in a living hell. All I want is our baby back."

He cradled her head against his chest. His whole world was collapsing around him and he could do nothing to put things right. Frustration seared his veins. He was tempted to go outside and give the journalists what for, but what good would that do? "Come on, love. I'll put some music on instead of the TV, how about that? At least, it'll drown out the noise of them talking outside."

"Okay, but it won't drive them away, will it? Why do they insist on badgering people who are suffering the worst loss imaginable? If Adele had died, at least we'd be sorting out her funeral right now. This is so much more traumatic. Or is it just me thinking that?"

"No, I feel it too, love. It's the not knowing. The inability to get out there and search for our baby, that's twisting my bloody insides to shreds." His gaze landed on the tray of food he'd prepared and he turned his nose up at the thought of trying to swallow down anything larger than the size of a pea, in case it got wedged in his throat by the constant lump that seemed to have embedded itself there. "Want me to get rid of this?"

"Yes, sorry. I just can't face it."

"You're not alone. I'll be right back." He took the tray into the kitchen and covered it over with a tea towel in case they changed their minds a little later. Martin returned to the living room on weary legs and plonked down onto the sofa next to Debs to comfort her.

Before long, the soothing music helped to relax them and they both drifted off to sleep, only to be woken by the doorbell ringing.

Martin leapt out of his seat and stormed across the room to peer out of the window, only to find a smartly dressed man and woman standing on the doorstep, ahead of the reporters. If he didn't know any better, he would have said the couple were police officers. He noticed the wary looks on the faces of the journalists who had backed up a little since their arrival.

He rushed through the house and opened the front door. The tall well-groomed male offered up his warrant card for him to study. "Mr Jenkins, I'm DI Lance Cooper and this is my partner, DS Karen Dorning. Would it be possible to chat inside?"

"Of course. I've been expecting you. DI Cobbs rang to explain she'd been in touch with you." Standing back, he gestured for them to enter. He secured the front door with the chain once more, then showed the detectives through to the living room and made the introductions to Debs.

"Have you heard something?" Debs asked, her hands clenched in her lap.

"I'm sorry, no. This visit is to introduce ourselves and to let you know that we're going to do everything we can to assist you," Lance replied.

Martin motioned for them to take a seat. "How will that work? Sorry, can I get you a drink?"

"No, don't go to any bother on our account. Of course, we realise that DI Cobbs will be in charge of the investigation up in The Lakes, that won't change. All we can do at this end is offer our support, as and when you need it."

"How will that manifest itself?"

"We'll be here to hold your hand. If, for instance, you get problems from the press, we can come along and help ease the stress."

"If that's the case, why are the press still out there, taking root on our doorstep then?" Martin queried, his temple pulled into a confused frown.

"I've had a word with them, told them at the first hint of trouble we'll come down here and force them to move on if necessary. In my experience, they'll get tired of hounding you soon enough, providing you don't react to them."

"I hope so. They're upsetting Debs, making this a darn sight more difficult to cope with."

Lance nodded. "I know. Hang in there. Their bosses will move them on soon enough, once another big story hits the headlines. Try to ignore them the best you can."

"I hope you're right. I know I spoke to the press before returning home, you know, while we were back in The Lakes, but I stupidly thought that would be the end of it. I presumed it would help our cause; instead, I feel it's hindered it." He ran a hand through his short hair and tugged it at the end.

"You felt it was the right thing at the time. I'm surprised DI Cobbs allowed you to do it and didn't advise you against giving an interview."

"Umm... I can't remember, I think she did advise against it, if I'm honest. Like everything else surrounding our daughter's disappearance, everything's hazy, to the point where it sometimes feels like we're in a dream and all this is happening to someone else. Or is that just wishful thinking on my part?"

"Others have said the same. Our hearts go out to you both. It's not an easy situation to deal with. We're going to do our best to ease the stress and strain on your shoulders. First though, I'm going to need to ask you a few questions, are you up for that?"

Martin gripped Debs' hand and nodded. "Of course. What do you want to know?"

DS Dorning withdrew her notebook and flipped it open. Once she was poised, ready to jot down the answers, DI Cooper asked his first question. "Just answer the best you can, okay? In recent months, have either of you noticed any strangers hanging around the house?"

Martin glanced in Debs' direction. She thought it over for a few seconds and then shook her head. "No."

"What about you, Martin?"

"No. I'm not sure if you're aware of our situation, but I'll fill you in, anyway. Debs and I were separated at the time of Adele's disappearance. I was on holiday with my daughter and my new girlfriend and her two children."

"I see. No, I wasn't aware of that fact. I'm glad you've got over your differences and have come back to support Deborah," Lance said, shifting uncomfortably in his seat.

"Oh no. We're back together again. You see, I blame my ex-girlfriend for not keeping an eye on Adele, who was in her care at the time."

Cooper inclined his head. "Really? May I ask where you were?"

He sighed heavily. "I was amusing Jake, her son, playing football with him. It was agreed that Louise would look after the two girls. Matilda, Louise's daughter, had something wrong with her, so Louise was seeing to her when Adele went missing."

"I see. That must have been a very traumatic experience for all of you to be confronted with."

"I know what you're thinking... I shouldn't have blamed Louise, and she's probably feeling like shit right now. You'd be right, but once Debs came to The Lakes... well, I realised that I still loved her and the rest is history. We should never have split up, Debs and Adele mean the world to me."

Lance tilted his head to the other side. "And yet you chose to leave them? Sorry if that sounds unsympathetic, I'm just trying to form a picture of the family dynamics in my head."

Martin smiled. "Yeah, you're not the only one. I was an idiot to leave my wife and child in the first place. Blame it on a man's egotistical need to feel wanted. None of it makes much sense when I say it out loud. It is what it is, I've made amends for my mistake, which has come at a cost neither of us was expecting or could ever imagine."

"And you, Deborah, can I ask how you feel about the situation?"

"I don't understand."

"Are you happy Martin is back home?"

"Of course I am. I'd be even happier if Adele was here with us as well. All we want now is for the police to find our daughter." She let out a gasp and clamped a hand over her mouth.

Martin twisted in his seat to face her, his heart racing as his fear rose. "What is it? What's wrong, Debs?"

"I've just had a thought. What if... umm... if someone took her and headed straight to the airport with our baby?"

Lance raised a hand. "I think that's highly unlikely. The culprit would have needed to have had a passport for your daughter in place before they attempted to abduct her. They would only have that if the abduction had been premeditated. Which, in my opinion, is unlikely, unless you have any proof to the contrary?"

Debs and Martin looked at each other and shook their heads. "No one we know would be capable of causing us this much pain," Martin said.

"On the one hand, that's a good thing. What about family? Are you in touch with everyone there? No conflicts at all?"

After chewing his lip while considering his answer, Martin replied, "I fell out with my mother a few months back, when I split up with Debs."

"Where does she live?"

"Here in Liverpool. But she's rung me twice since Adele went missing. She said she saw me making a plea to the public on the TV and decided to get in touch. Actually, my sister Morgan rang me first and I was a little short with her. Mum called to chastise me. You know what mothers are like when a family falls out."

"Do you believe either of them is capable of snatching Adele?"

Martin scratched his head and stared at the two detectives. "No. I really don't. Like I said, we haven't been in touch for months and they only contacted me once the story aired." He turned to look at Debs. "What do you think?"

She shrugged and shook her head. "I can't see it. But who knows?"

Martin left his seat and paced the floor a few times, heaved out a sigh, then sank onto the sofa again. "Oh God, you've got me thinking now. Will you go and question them? Or should I go?"

Lance raised a hand. "Let's not do anything rash. We'll see to it, as part of our enquiries. What about you, Debs? Do you have any family members who are likely to have taken Adele?"

"No. Sadly, I'm all alone. My parents died within a few years of each other when I was younger and I don't have any siblings."

Fresh tears dripped onto her cheeks, and Martin flung a comforting arm around her shoulder. "It's okay, love. He had to ask."

She sniffled. "I know. It doesn't stop the pain from resurfacing. I wish Mum and Dad were here to offer their support when we need it the most."

"Sorry, I didn't mean to upset you. Okay, let's leave that for now. Martin we'll need the addresses of both your mother and your sister before we go. Let's move on, can I ask what jobs you both have?"

"I'm a sales manager for an import and export firm. Debs doesn't work, Adele has only just started primary school, she's still settling in."

"It's difficult finding a job in the current climate, if you've been off for the past few years, looking after your child. I'm hoping that will change soon… if she ever comes home," Debs added.

"She will, love," Martin assured her, gripping her hand once more.

"And with your firm, Martin, can you cast your mind back a few months to anything that might have angered someone you've recently done business with?"

"No, not at all. I get on well with all my clients. They say I've got the gift of the gab, but I'm super friendly with it. I've never once got annoyed with a customer, ever. So there's no reason to suspect anyone of doing this to me, to us."

"I have to ask this, please forgive me if you believe I'm way off the mark. Your export business is above board?"

"Crikey, yes, definitely. Wayne is a much-respected businessman.

He's the owner. He prides himself on being an utter professional and only employs people, such as myself, who treat the business in the same way."

"That's good to know. There are so many dodgy haulage and export companies around at the moment, who are intent on trafficking people into the country. It's mind-blowing, as you can imagine. It's also getting harder to enforce with our limited funds."

"Ah yes, I understand what you're getting at now. Yes, we're aware of what's going on in this country. We've been shafted a number of times by such companies, but Wayne has always taken the moral high ground and risen above the threats he's had to deal with."

Cooper's intrigue piqued. "Wait, your boss has been threatened in the past? Has anything come of those threats?"

Saliva filled Martin's mouth. "Umm... not as far as I know. You don't think...?"

"It's a possibility, one we'd be foolish to ignore at this stage. I'll need to chase things up with your boss, Wayne, you said?"

"Yes, Wayne Turnbull. I'll get you his number now."

"The address of the business would be preferable. I'd much rather interview him face to face, if possible."

"Of course, I can supply you with that. Oh, God, the connotations of this could be far reaching, couldn't they?"

"They always are during any investigation. Which is why it's always advisable for people to tell us the truth, and provide us with all the facts no matter how insignificant those facts may seem at the time. It's surprising where things lead to in the end."

"I can understand that now. Oh, God, the thought of Adele getting caught up in something as sinister as people trafficking." He raked his hand through his hair again. "I can't even comprehend how bad that could be. No, correction, I refuse to even think about it."

Cooper shook his head and smiled. "Then don't. You leave the worrying to us, okay? The last thing I wanted to do was heap more stress and anxiety on your shoulders."

"I'll try and ignore it for now, it's not going to be easy, though."

"I know. Is there anything else you think we should know before we go? What about you, Deborah?" DS Dorning asked. "Any hassle at the school gates? Anything along those lines that you believe we should be delving into?"

"No. I truly can't think of anything. I get on well with all the mothers, and the odd father, who drop their children off at primary school."

"That's good to hear. We can cross them off our list of suspects then. Okay, I think we've covered everything now. If you can give us the three addresses, we'll be on our way."

DS Dorning handed Martin her notebook. He looked up the addresses for his mother and sister and wrote them on a clean sheet of paper, then added his work address. Passing it back, he smiled. "Mum's and Morgan's, plus my work address. I take it you don't want me to ring ahead and warn them that you're going to be in touch?"

"No, not advisable. If either one of them is involved, us showing up unannounced will send them into a panic. We know what to look out for. I'm going to leave you my card. Please, ring me day or night if you need to speak to me, or if you think of anything else we need to speak about."

Martin rose to his feet, took the proffered card and placed it on the sideboard on his way out into the passage. At the front door, he shook both the detectives' hands. "Is there any chance you can have a word with the press? They're only making the situation worse."

"I'll see what I can do. Keep your heads low, try not to leave the house. They've been known to follow people and cause all sorts of mayhem in the process."

"We're staying put for now. No need for us to go out. I'm still on holiday at the moment and the cupboards are pretty well stocked up."

"Good. I'll be in touch soon, should I uncover anything of importance during the interviews."

"Thank you."

As soon as Martin opened the door he was blinded by flashes and the journalists all jostled to get a better look at him. He tucked himself behind the door and listened to DI Cooper exerting his authority over the ravenous pack.

"Get back. You guys need to show this couple the respect they deserve. Don't you think they're going through enough at the moment? Why do you persist in making their lives a bloody misery? Have some heart for a change. Go on, get back. You have no right encroaching on their personal space at this unbearable time." Cooper and Dorning pushed through the pack. Cooper took a swipe at one of the journalists who rammed a camera in his face, bashing him on the nose. "Right, I've given you fair warning. Either you stand back ten yards or I call for backup and start arresting some of you. Maybe you'll listen then. What's it to be? The decision is yours."

A few of them shifted backwards, but most of them stood their ground in a defiant stance. Todd Wilkins cleared his throat and shouted, "We have a right to be here. The public are interested in this case. If you can persuade the parents to speak to us, then we'd leave immediately, Inspector. You, of all people, know how these things work."

"And you, Wilkins, are the lowest of the low. If the parents wanted to chat with you, they would have done it by now."

Martin had heard enough. He straightened his shoulders and emerged from his hiding place behind the door to confront them. "If that's what it will take to get rid of you. Here it is. My beautiful daughter has gone missing; we're presuming she has been abducted. Two kind inspectors and their teams are doing their best for us to get our daughter back. I'm pleading with you not to hamper their progress in any way. Answer me this, how would you feel if it was your child who had been taken? Bear that little nugget in mind. Thank you, that's all I have to say. Now kindly leave us alone." He firmly shut the door and stood behind it until his heart rate slowed down.

Debs came into the hallway and found him in the same position a few minutes later. "Everything all right, Martin? Did someone hurt you? Say anything to you?"

"All's fine. I gave them what they wanted in the hope they would leave us alone, but it knocked me for six. I was just catching my breath again." He nudged away from the door, took a look through the spyhole and let out a relieved sigh. "I think it's worked."

"Oh, I do hope so. Not sure I could have coped with them hounding us for much longer."

He noticed her hands shaking. He stepped forward and wrapped his arms around her and whispered, "I'll always be by your side, protecting you, sweetheart."

"I'm glad to hear it. I love you so much, Martin."

10

Five Years Later

"Jackie, can you get me the file for the Hawker contract?"

"Yes, Mr Jenkins, right away, sir." The older woman scurried out of the office and returned, all beaming smiles and shaking hands as she deposited the file on his desk, spilling most of the contents in her urgency to please him. "Here you are, sir. Oops! Can I get you anything else?"

"Not for the moment. Shut the door on your way out, if you would." He was desperate for a coffee, but her enthusiasm to please him had already cost him a packet in dry cleaning bills this month. He'd give her a couple of weeks, see if she settled down a little. If there was no improvement by then, he'd be forced to make yet another change. In the past five years, since Louise had left the firm, he'd failed to find a suitable replacement for her. Jackie was the last in a very long line of secretaries who were definitely not up to the task. Working with Louise had been effortless at the time. Maybe that's why he'd found her attractive and ended up having an affair with her.

His gaze drifted out of the window, and the urgent matter of chasing up a shipment that had gone missing was temporarily forgotten. He wondered, not for the first time, how Louise and her two kids were getting on. He'd found himself more and more tempted lately to ring her to find out, stopping himself at the last moment, fearing where it might lead again. He directed his thoughts to Debs instead.

Life was still tough for him and Debs, even though they were new parents to an adorable little boy called Logan who was three months old. He would never replace Adele, who was still missing, but he gave them something to focus on, rather than trawling the internet day in day out for any likely sightings of their beautiful daughter.

Five years of hell they had been through. In that time, Debs had never returned to work; her nerves were badly frayed and beyond repair. They hadn't planned on having another child either, although Logan had turned out to be a blessing in disguise. The news they were expecting a child had given Debs hope, but when Logan had arrived Debs was a little deflated. She'd clearly been hoping for a girl. This revelation meant she'd taken a turn for the worse mentally.

Life had been exceptionally hard for both of them. Debs struggling to cope with Logan, and him finding himself overstretched at work with a bunch of new clients to handle as the business swiftly expanded. He was now working far longer hours, just when Debs needed him the most. Again, his inability to return to the house before eight o'clock at night had put a vast amount of stress on their relationship. In truth, he was feeling penned in, to the point of suffocation.

At times, he was grateful that work was full on. It distracted him long enough to forget about what his life had become. There were days when he didn't even think about Adele, as heartless as that might sound to an outsider. She was there, still in his heart and in his mind at the weekends when he had no work to contend with, but during the week, he devoted all his excess energy to his work.

Unlike Debs.

She was at home, caring for Logan and making comparisons between the two children all day long. Adele had been a happy baby, but Logan was the total opposite—he cried most days, even during the night, to the extent that neither of them got much rest. It was all too draining for Debs, and he felt for her; but then, at least she could put her feet up during the day and catch a nap when Logan finally gave his lungs a rest. He couldn't.

He rang home, the guilt playing havoc with his conscience. "How are you, Debs?"

"Bad today. Listen to him, he hasn't bloody stopped since you left this morning. I'm not cut out to be a mother. First, my daughter goes missing, and now my son wants nothing to do with me. The second I pick him up for a cuddle, he starts bawling again. I want my life back, Martin, the carefree life I had before he came along."

"Debs, don't think that way. He'll settle down soon. Did you call the midwife?"

"Yes, she can't get to me for a few days, I'm in a damn queue, can you believe that?"

"Did you explain how you're feeling?"

"Yes, she told me it's normal for a newborn to cry all the time. I know that's a load of bullshit. She's fobbing me off as if I'm a brand-new mother who hasn't been through this before."

"Can you demand a new midwife? Ask for someone else to come and see you?"

"No. They told me there's a shortage in the area."

"God, I'm sorry, love. I wish I knew what to say or do to help."

"Can't you take a day off? That would help me out."

He groaned. "I wish I could, but Wayne has me stretched in all directions. He's invested millions in the business and is finally reaping the rewards with the number of new clients knocking on the door."

"Can't he employ extra staff to cope with the influx? Why should you be made to work extra hours every day?" She sniffled.

"Debs, try not to get upset. I'll have a word with him. See if I can sort out another holiday soon. How's that?"

"Yes, yes, then we could go away and maybe someone will abduct Logan, with any luck."

"Jesus, I can't believe you said that. What the fuck were you thinking, flinging that in my face?"

Debs broke down and his guilt gene prodded him with a stick. "I'm sorry. I wasn't thinking. I would never wish that on him," she said, between sobs.

"It's all right. I know how difficult things are for you at the moment. Do you want me to hire someone to help out, a nanny perhaps? I think we can stretch to one if we cut back elsewhere."

"No. That would only highlight what a failure I've become."

"Nonsense. Of course it wouldn't. If I get the chance today, I'll ring around a few agencies, all right? Unless you want to do it for me?"

"I can't. I never get a moment's peace to make a damn phone call."

"Okay, leave it with me. Keep your chin up, love. We'll sort this out, and soon."

"I'll try." Logan's crying notched up a level in the background. Martin cringed and hung up.

While he had every sympathy with Debs, he didn't have a clue how to make the situation better. He jotted down a note on his pad to remind himself to call a few agencies in his lunch break, if he got one.

꩜

*D*ebs fed Logan, but he refused the milk she offered him from her breast. She began expressing it in the hope that would make a difference, but it didn't. "What the hell am I supposed to do? Why won't you eat or sleep? What have I done to deserve this? I can't cope. Not any more." She crumpled onto the sofa and tucked the baby on the other end against the back, away from the edge. His crying ceased for a few minutes until he got used to his position and started bawling all over again. She clamped her hands over her ears and shouted, "Stop it! Stop! No more! This is too much! I need to rest!"

Still, Logan cried. Soon she was crying alongside him. "What am I doing wrong? Why won't you just stop bloody crying? Why do you hate me so much? Why? Why? Why?"

She sat up and stared at her son. His tiny features were screwed up in anger and discomfort. She switched on the app on her phone, and a soothing lullaby filled the room, but it did nothing to quell Logan's crying.

Debs checked him over for any signs of him hurting. That was the trouble with babies, they couldn't tell you if they were in pain. After stripping him off, she found nothing, no tell-tale signs that anything was wrong on his skin. So why was he constantly crying, driving her insane? Was this God's way of punishing her? His way of ensuring she never had another day's rest in her life after what happened to Adele?

She picked Logan up and took him upstairs to the bathroom. She ran the bath, making sure it was cool enough for him to lie in, then she placed him in the tub. His crying magically stopped. Kneeling down, she smiled and bathed him. He kicked his little legs in the water and even reciprocated her smile now and again, which made her heart sing. "Maybe you're a water baby, a boy who prefers to spend most of his time in the bath." She tested her theory by lifting him out of the water. Logan instantly screwed his face up and started crying again. She placed him back in the water and his crying stopped. Well, at least she'd had a breakthrough, of sorts. But how the hell did she handle the situation going forward? She couldn't leave him in the bath indefinitely, he'd be shrivelled and probably develop gills and scales before long. She shuddered at the thought of spending hour upon hour in the cold bathroom during the winter months.

After bathing Logan, she got him dressed and placed him back in his cot while she showered and dressed herself. An idea sparked. Maybe a trip to the park will help, a little fresh air might do wonders for him and help settle him down.

Twenty minutes later, she placed Logan in the pram and set off to the park at the end of their road. There was a lake there, maybe he'd stop crying if he watched the ducks frolicking in the water.

Standing by the edge of the lake, she took her crying son out of the pram and pointed at the ducks, bobbing about on the water. At first, his cries intensified. Was that because she was holding him? After a while, his focus became drawn to the birds and he began to kick his legs in happiness.

"Lovely to see them so engrossed at that age," a passer-by said.

Debs smiled at the woman. "I needed something to distract him. He won't stop crying, it's driving me nuts."

The older woman came closer and smiled at Logan. "My grandson was just the same. Have you tried going on car journeys with the little mite?"

"I've tried everything. I think I had a breakthrough moment this morning. I put him in the bath and he stopped crying straight away. Once I took him out, he started up again." *What am I doing, talking to a perfect stranger like this? Don't be ridiculous!*

"Oh dear, he's a water baby, obviously. So you thought you'd bring him here to look at the ducks on the lake. That was a great idea."

The kindness in the woman's tone put her at ease. "I've run out of ideas, this was my last shot. I can't stay here all day though, can I?"

"What about getting a paddling pool for the garden? You do have a garden, don't you, dear?"

"Yes, that's a brilliant suggestion. I'll order one off the internet today. Thank you so much for your help." She felt relieved to be speaking with this woman who clearly had years of experience behind her.

"It's no problem. Have you thought about joining a Mother and Baby club? How old is he?"

"He's only three months. No, I haven't, I'm a little rusty about things like that. Do you think they help?"

"Undoubtedly, they'll offer the support you need to cope with the tears and temper tantrums. They're sure to follow the crying stage, in my experience." She chuckled. "Something to look forward to, eh? There should be one around here somewhere, would you like me to check on my phone for you?"

Debs jiggled her son up and down, doing her best to keep him quiet a while longer. "Would you? That would be so kind of you. I'll be forever in your debt. I've had a nightmare of a time with him lately. I think I've possibly reached my limit."

"We'll get you sorted. Hang in there. All mothers feel that way now and again. Let me have a look for you." The woman scrolled through her phone and then typed something in. "Ah, yes, here we are, The

Gingerbread Club." She jabbed a thumb over her shoulder. "Down that road there, if I'm not mistaken, I've passed it many a time out on a walk."

"That's fantastic. I'll take a detour, drop in on my way back home. I can't thank you enough for stopping and talking to me."

"You're most welcome. Can't bear to see a new mother struggling."

"My first child was an absolute gem, compared to this monkey."

"Aww… I'm sure you're the perfect mother. There are some women who wouldn't bother bringing their son out for a visit to the park. You're to be congratulated, dear, at least you're trying to address the problem. What about your midwife, no luck there?"

"She's rushed off her feet. Short staffed, apparently."

"To be expected after the pandemic, a lot of lockdown babies being born, I suppose."

"I never thought about that. Yes, you're probably right. Thank you again for your help."

"No problem. Maybe I'll see you around here again one day. I quite often cut through on my way into town."

"I'll look out for you in the future." Debs waved and smiled as the woman set off. She returned her attention to her son and pointed at the ducks gathering by the riverbank, about to hop out of the water. He gurgled and smiled. A completely different child to the one she'd been living a tormented life with for the past three months. They stayed there for the next hour. She placed Logan in and out of his pram at regular intervals before drifting around the lake for a different view to keep him amused. Finally, Logan fell asleep, and Debs took the opportunity to head off in the direction of The Ginger-bread Club.

At the end of a row of terraced houses, she located the prefab-type building that was set in a concrete playground. Debs opened the door and was greeted by a young woman with a friendly smile on her pretty face. She had a small child hanging off one leg and was holding another in her arms. They looked identical.

"Hi, I'm after a little advice really."

"Come in, take a seat. I'll close the door. I'm used to having these two clinging to me all day long."

"Are they yours?"

"Unfortunately, yes." She smirked.

"Twins?"

"Yep, how can you tell?" The woman laughed. "I'm Monica, by the way."

"Deborah, sorry, Debs. And this is Logan. He's asleep right now, which is a rarity for him, I can assure you."

"Ah, one of the world's biggest criers, is he?"

"You could say that," Debs replied. She instantly felt relaxed talking to the woman. *Maybe this will be a good place to visit after all.*

"Now then, how can I help?" Monica placed the children on the activity mat beside her and sat behind the reception desk.

"I was wondering if you have an opening for me."

"Usually, I'd say no, but you're in luck. One of our ladies has just moved out of the area and left an opening. How old is your son?"

"He's only three months old. I need something to stimulate him, I think. I've had a terrible couple of months, but had a eureka moment this morning when I figured out putting him in a warm bath seemed to help."

"Ah, that old trick, yes, it works wonders. Glad you finally discovered something to ease your stress. These two were a bloody nightmare when they were younger."

"Ouch, double the trouble, eh?"

"Yes, indeed. Anyway, enough about me. Let's get some information down and I'll give you a pack to take away with you. Mull it over, see if it's the sort of thing you're looking for and then come back to me."

"What are the charges?"

"We try to keep things cheap around here. It's currently four pounds fifty for a two-hour stint. That's usually enough for the children and the parents alike. Does that sound all right for you?"

"Yes, I think I can manage that okay. I'll cut back on the shopping for a week or so."

The woman smiled. "That's the ticket. Hubby won't know any different, will he?"

"No, not that he's home much to notice, anyway. He works exceptionally long hours, leaving me to handle the baby most days on my own."

Monica wrinkled her nose. "So you don't get any reprieve, is that it?"

"Yes, it's not his fault, I'm not blaming him."

"I know, I didn't take it that way. If he's the breadwinner, then needs must, right? We've all been there. My hubby works shifts, it's not easy for either of us, especially with these two on the go all the time. This place has been an absolute godsend to us, as a family."

"That's wonderful to hear."

"Why don't I show you around? You don't have to decide today; you might think it's not worth the money, although I assure you it is. The support you receive is second to none, I promise you."

"Thanks, I'd like that." Logan woke up, Debs swooped him up into her arms.

"Let me ask Janet to mind these two for me for five minutes, I'll be right back."

Monica picked up her two children and walked into another room off to the left. She returned childless a few seconds later and gestured for Debs to join her. "Right, this is where we all gather and hang out when the kids are all distracted enough to be left, for a few minutes' breather. There's a vending machine over in the corner there. Some of the ladies love to bake and often bring in homemade treats. We all get along great, I think you're going to fit in here, and Logan will gobble up the interaction, which in the end will make your life so much more bearable."

Debs smiled. "I feel much more relaxed already." She jigged Logan on her hip and said, "You're going to love it here, little man, aren't you?" His eyes were everywhere, taking in all the bright colours on the walls and on the floor around him.

"He seems to be very aware of his surroundings, that usually indicates their need to explore. Does he have many toys at home?" Monica held up a hand and chuckled. "I know, dumb question. All babies are inundated with a lot of toys from friends and family, right?"

"He's got a few, not many, to be honest. Maybe that's the problem. I should get him some more, if you think the stimulation will help?"

"My advice would be not to spend out too much just yet. Once you join the club, you can take note of which toys he prefers to play with and go from there, it'll save you money in the long run. I'm all for doing that, toys can be exceptionally pricey nowadays."

"Good call. Thanks for the tip."

"I'm full of them. Hubby would say I'm full of something, but it's usually followed by something derogatory."

Debs sniggered. "Men, eh? Can't live with them and can't live without them."

"Yeah, even that's debatable at times. I'll take you through to the sun room, it's where we spend most of our time, if I'm honest with you. Nothing brightens the day more than feeling a little warmth on your back, does it?" Monica led the way into a large room made of glass. It opened out onto the playground area she'd seen at the front. "We generally leave the doors open so the kids can come in and out as they please."

Horrified at the prospect of the kids being out there on their own, Debs asked, "Don't you have to keep an eye on them?"

"Definitely, all the time. There are mothers on duty everywhere around here, plus three members of staff."

"That's reassuring. I'm getting a good feel for this place, can't wait to sign up." She hugged Logan, and he squirmed in her arms. "I think this place is going to suit you down to the ground, Logan."

"It will, I promise. We have a few children around his age. I know he'll be too young to let out of your sight just yet, but I'm sure you're both going to make friends soon enough. Everyone is super welcoming and friendly around here."

"Sounds ideal, just what we need. It gets boring being at home all day by yourself, there's only so much housework you can do."

"That's true enough. Talking of which, if Logan is a crier, how does he react to the vacuum cleaner or washing machine being used?"

"He hates the vacuum, I try not to use it that much, not unless hubby is at home to watch Logan for me. As for the washing machine, I can't say I've really noticed. What's with that?"

"One of the ladies shared with the group a few months ago that she couldn't get her daughter to settle, so she put the baby in her basket near the washing machine and it worked wonders. Sent the child to sleep right away. She did some research on the internet and read that apparently the machine's noise reminds babies of when they were in the womb."

"Oh my, how interesting. I'll be sure to try it. I'm learning so much already."

"Free advice, too, nothing better in this world than that, I can assure you. Okay, that's about it, apart from the main room. I'll take you in there if you want me to introduce you to everyone. I don't want you to feel overwhelmed, though, so no pressure from me."

"No, I'd love to. I'm really keen to meet everyone."

Monica wove her way back through the tiny tables and chairs dotted about the room and entered the final destination on the right. As soon as the door opened, everyone turned their way. Normally, Debs would have flinched by all the unwelcome attention—not a good socialite—however, the smiles on the women's faces made her feel relaxed and eager to get to know them all. She waved. "Hi, everyone. This is Logan and I'm Debs, I'm so pleased to meet you all."

Monica tugged her arm gently. "Come on, I'll introduce you to everyone."

They circulated the room, and Debs marvelled at Logan who seemed at ease in his surroundings. She set him on the floor to play with a few of the younger children. He smiled and waved his arms, unable to do much else at his age. It was a pure relief not to hear him bawling all the time.

"Have you seen enough now?" Monica asked.

"Oh yes, I think we're going to fit in really well. Thanks ever so much, to all of you for making me and Logan feel so welcome."

They went back to the reception area where Monica gave Debs an information pack. "The number is on there, just give us a ring once you've talked it over with hubby."

"Umm... I don't need to. When can I come?"

Monica laughed. "You're keen. What about tomorrow?"

"That would be brilliant. What time?"

"Can you get here for nine or soon after?"

"Of course. I'll go back home and do some housework, save doing it tomorrow."

"Sounds like you have everything organised. We'll look forward to seeing you then. Stay until one, or go sooner, it's up to you, it'll be somewhat challenging the first few days, it's always the same when you start somewhere new, isn't it?"

"I'll take that on board. Should I bring anything with me?"

"Just the usual baby things, you know, for changing Logan and perhaps a drink and sandwich if you think you'll need one. Saying that, there's bound to be some form of goodies on offer. What is it tomorrow? Ah, yes, Wednesday, Janet usually bakes on Tuesdays and brings us the results to ensure we keep up our calories."

"Ouch, okay. I'm not much of a baker, but I'll get some practice in at the weekend, if I can."

"No pressure. I'd better rescue my two little buggers now. See you in the morning and welcome aboard, Debs. You're going to love it here."

Debs waved goodbye and settled Logan in his pram. She left the building, feeling like a heavy burden had been lifted from her shoulders. The walk home took no time at all and appeared to have been achieved on autopilot. She got to work after she'd placed Logan into his Moses basket. He seemed to be a different child, more at peace with the world.

Over the next few hours, she worked hard to prepare two meals, one for that evening's dinner and the second for the following day, taking on board Monica's suggestion that she would probably be exhausted after her first day. Then she cleaned the house from top to bottom until it was gleaming. The visit to The Gingerbread Club had given her a new impetus in life.

During the afternoon, she created a new play area for Logan and searched through his toys to see if there was anything bright and cheerful, similar to those she'd seen at the club as she felt that would stimulate him. Only a few met with her approval, so she spent ten minutes or so trawling through a well-known online shopping site for more ideas. She placed several items in her trolley with the intention of showing them to Martin later, once Logan was tucked up in bed for the night.

She collected Logan from his basket, fed and changed him, then put on some music and found herself dancing around the lounge with him. She was amazed he hadn't cried at all since they'd got back.

By the time Martin came home at around eight, she'd put Logan to bed and dinner was waiting for him on the table. He held her in his arms and kissed her. "Everything all right?"

"Fine. How was your day?"

"The same as always. Hey, you seem more cheerful than I've seen you in a long time. Has something happened?"

"I'll tell you about it over dinner. Do you want to get washed up? I've cooked your favourite, lasagne."

"You've mentioned the magic word. I'll be back in a jiffy. I'm starving."

He tore upstairs and was back down within five minutes, changed out of his suit into a casual pair of jeans and T-shirt. "I popped my head into the nursery, he's sparko." Debs dished up the lasagne and salad and handed him a plate. "Are you going to tell me why there's a noticeable difference in you?"

She smiled, finished dishing up her own dinner then sat down next to him. "I've finally found the solution to Logan's constant crying." She went over the details of how she'd obtained the revelation and informed him about the club, then watched carefully for his reaction. He laid down his knife and fork and took a sip of his orange juice. "Well, say something."

"Like what? You've obviously made up your mind, you don't need my approval, do you?"

"It would be nice if you gave it, though. Do you think I'm doing the right thing?"

"Oh, definitely, sorry if it sounded otherwise. How was Logan there?"

"A different child. Umm... I was wondering if we could stretch to buying him some more toys, ones that would help to stimulate him."

"I don't see why not. I'm due a bonus at the end of the month, it's yours, spend it how you like."

"I love you, you're the greatest husband ever to walk this planet."

He chuckled. "Yeah, I know. Don't spread it around down at the club, they'll all be wanting a piece of me."

"No way, no woman is ever going to get their claws into you in the future. I'll put up a bloody fight next time."

He shook his head. "I'm sorry, Debs, for ever straying, it wasn't intentional. Hey, to make sure it doesn't happen again, I'm being extra careful with whom I take on in the future. The last thing I want to do is cause you to have major doubts."

"Really? I didn't know that. You didn't have to. I'm not as insecure as I used to be, at least, I don't think I am. I trust you, Martin. We're happy again, aren't we?"

"Basically, I know things have been a little fraught since Logan came along, but at the end of the day, our love is far stronger than it used to be."

"When you started the affair, you mean?"

He winced. "Yes, okay, I agree, back before my infidelity struck."

"Sorry, I didn't mean to make you squirm. I won't bring it up again."

"Good. Let's rephrase it to say 'before we got back together', how's that? Anyway, setting that aside for now, I'm glad you've discovered a club that will be beneficial for both of you. I have to say, I've been worried sick about your mental state, being stuck at home with grumpy Logan, that can't be fun for you."

"I had doubts there myself for a while. Let's hope this is the turning point we need to make our family a happy unit once more. I can't wait to join tomorrow. I'm going to be as nervous as hell, but I can't see that lasting for long. Everyone seemed super friendly."

Relieved and happy to see Debs excited about something new and that her being around others would ease his concerns, he hugged her and said, "Good. You need to get out more and see people with a few of the same interests to talk to. I couldn't hack what you do all day."

"I appreciate you saying that. Some days are definitely better than others. Still, it was my choice. I love being a mum."

He raised her hand to his lips and kissed the back of it. "I know you do, love. Eat up, let's not get all maudlin. What's for pudding?"

"Crikey, I didn't do one…"

"I'm joking. I'll be stuffed after I've wolfed down this lot. Thank you for taking care of us both so well."

"That's my role, isn't it?"

"No, we're a partnership. You look after Logan all day and look at this place, it's spotless. I bet there aren't many homes around which look this good with a three-month-old in residence."

Debs laughed. "I went the extra mile, thought it would save me a job tomorrow, you know, take the pressure off a bit."

"What pressure? There's never any pressure from me, sweetheart."

"I know." She pointed at her temple. "My own demons never let it rest, though. I'm so lucky to have such an understanding husband as you."

"Yep, glad we agree on that."

She smiled and took a swipe at his hand, but he retracted it quickly.

11

*D*ebs sat on the sofa in her coat and shoes the next morning, clock-watching until it read eight-forty-five, then she tucked Logan into his pram and set off. Her nerves jangled, inter-twining with the excitement.

Debs ended up being five minutes early. Monica was ever cheerful and there to welcome her. The other women took their seats and one of them patted the chair next to her and invited Debs to sit.

"Hi, I was here yesterday. I'm Emmy; Emma really, but I hate it."

"Pleased to meet you. I'm the same with my name, Deborah, it sounds so formal. Have you been coming here long? Which one of these monsters is yours?"

"The one with wheat-coloured hair." Emmy pointed at the relevant child.

"What a lovely way to describe her hair. It's gorgeous."

"That's Cilla, my little princess. We named her after Cilla Black, lovely lady. I met her once."

"Did you? Where?"

"I was on that show of hers back in the nineties, *Blind Date*."

"Wow! No way. How cool. I used to watch it every Saturday. Did you end up with anyone?"

"Sadly yes, but he turned out to be a womanising jerk. I dumped him, remained single for two years and when I wasn't expecting it, my husband Richard walked into my life and a baby was the result of our first time in the sack together. Sorry, too much information, I'm always doing that."

Debs snorted. "Oh heck, that's hilarious. Or was it? It could have put a tremendous strain on your relationship from the outset."

"Yeah, it could have, but luckily it didn't, we got through it. Richard is one in a million. He adores kids, we have five now."

"Blimey! That's a handful to have to contend with every day."

"We're in a routine, good job, as they get older, the more arguments they have between them."

"I can imagine. What ages are they?"

"Let's see if I can remember… that sounds awful, but a couple have recently had their birthdays. Sixteen, fourteen, twelve, ten, and Cilla who is three. Go on, now ask me why there's such a large gap."

"All right, if you insist, why the gap?"

Debs waited with anticipation.

"I had breast cancer in between and, to be honest, we were told we'd probably never conceive again, so we stopped using bloody contraceptives and nine months later, out pops Missy over there."

"Oh no, I'm so sorry. About the cancer. That must have been a huge shock to deal with and then having a baby on top, what a nightmare to have to deal with."

"It was. We ended up having to buy a new house—the old one was packed full to the rafters, which means that Richard has to work more hours to cover the extra mortgage we needed."

"Ouch, not good, eh? My Martin works long hours as well. Not so good when you have five kids to manage on your own, how do you cope?"

"We have a rota system, I make sure the children all help out. Luckily, they're all girls so there's no quibbles, as such. I think it'll stand them in good stead, ready for what lies ahead of them in the distant future; I hope they don't start too soon, not sure I could bear having grandkids running around the place, not for a few years. Maybe when Cilla is off our hands eventually, I'll feel differently. Until such a time, no thank you. Anyway, I've said far too much already. What about you? Is Logan your only child?"

She smiled, surprised Emmy had remembered Logan's name from the day before. "He is... umm... although, I had a daughter ten years ago."

"Oh no, did you lose her? No, stop, you don't have to share something so personal with me, you hardly know me."

"Honestly, it's fine. Yes, we literally lost her, or more to the point, someone stole her from us."

Emmy hissed and covered her mouth. After a few seconds she dropped her hand. "Oh my, that has to be every parent's worst nightmare. I'm so very sorry you had to go through that ordeal. I take it the police were involved."

"Yes, two forces, one up in The Lakes, where the incident occurred and the force down here. We've been forgotten about for years. The police stopped updating us a few years ago. It's so hard when that happens. As far as we know, Adele is still out there. Until we hear differently, that's what we're going to carry on believing."

Emmy squeezed her hand in support. "Quite right, too. I feel for you. Is there anything else I can do to help?"

"No. It's kind of you to offer. I had depression for a few years until Logan came along; there are some days when he drives me to distraction with his incessant crying, but most of the time, well, I wouldn't be without him."

"Hey, all children tick us off at some time or the other."

"I know. Coming here is going to save my sanity, I think."

*O*ver the next few weeks, Debs attended The Gingerbread Club twice a week. She paid for one outing, and Martin paid for her second visit; she counted herself fortunate to have his support. Every time she attended the club, she spent more and more time with Emmy and they became firm friends. One day in particular, Emmy invited her back to her place for a spot of afternoon tea. They enjoyed coffee and cream cakes and chatted like pals who'd known each other for years.

"Right, I suppose I'd better get my finger out and pick up the children, correction, two of them. They're at separate schools, you see. All within walking distance, of course. I hate using the car for short trips. I'm trying my best to be environmentally friendly where possible." Emmy giggled.

"I'm trying, it's not always possible though, not in our house."

"Why don't you come with me? Logan's asleep, the movement in the pram will help keep him relaxed for a while, giving you some much needed me-time."

Excitement grew in Debs, it was lovely of Emmy to offer to include her. "Would you mind? I'd love to meet your children."

"Come on then, if we get a wriggle on, we can have a nice leisurely walk instead of the frantic one that usually takes place every day in my world."

They strolled through the local park on the way to St Saviour's Primary School to pick up Gina, Emmy's ten-year-old daughter. The kids were just coming out of the gate when they got there. Most of them came hurtling towards the parents, waiting for them. Gina was one of the first to leave the school playground. She bolted at Emmy and flung herself into her mother's open arms. "Hello, darling. Have you had a good day?"

"The best, Mummy. Who's she?" Gina asked, peering over her mother's shoulder at Debs.

Emmy put Gina on the ground, straightened up and tucked a few stray hairs behind her daughter's right ear. "Gina, I'd like you to meet a good friend of mine, this is Debs."

"Hello, pleased to meet you," Gina said, her impeccable manners coming easily without Emmy needing to prompt her.

"It's wonderful to finally meet you too, Gina."

Gina leaned over the pram, saw Logan was asleep and whispered, "How old is he or she?"

"Logan is a terror of a boy and he's coming up to four months old."

"Babies are so cute. I want ten of them when I grow up."

"You do? That's news to me," Emmy spluttered, her eyes wide, either from the shock or in horror at the thought.

Debs suppressed a giggle. "That's nice, good luck with your ambition. Babies are a lot of hard work."

Gina bent down and picked up her little sister, Cilla, and kissed her lots of times all over her face. "Yes, but they're adorable. Aren't you, Cilla?"

Cilla squealed and hugged her sister's neck tightly. Eventually, Gina popped her sister back on her feet again and clutched her hand.

Emmy beamed with delight, and Debs could see how much the children loved one another which clawed at her insides and made her wish that Adele was here to play with her little brother and see him grow up.

A hand touched her arm. "Are you all right, Debs?"

Debs swallowed down the lump filling her throat and smiled. "Sorry, just thinking of what-ifs, you know?"

"I do. I'm sorry, I should have thought about that before bringing you here today."

She waved the suggestion away. "Don't be daft. I've loved meeting Gina, she's such a special little girl. You're truly blessed to have..." Her voice trailed off as she caught sight of a little girl waiting at the gates. The girl spotted Debs staring at her and dropped her gaze to look at the pavement. Debs was eager to get closer. There was something about the little girl which seemed familiar.

"Debs, what's wrong?"

"I... umm... I don't know."

Emmy followed her gaze. "Do you know her?"

"Do you?" Debs was quick to respond.

"Gina, who's that little girl standing by the gate?"

"Oh, that's Susie Withers, she joined us at the start of last term."

"Do you know where she was before that?" Debs asked, unable to take her eyes off the child.

"A school on the other side of Liverpool, I think. Want me to ask for you?"

"Oh, no, it's all right. I was just curious, I thought I recognised her for a minute. I must be mistaken."

Emmy frowned, but then announced, "We'd better get going, Lilly will be coming out of school soon. She goes nuts if I'm late. Are you coming, Debs?"

"Of course." Debs followed Gina, Cilla and Emmy as they marched up the road. Now and again, Debs found herself glancing over her shoulder to find the girl watching her. Once they turned the corner at the top of the road and the girl was no longer in sight, Debs couldn't help feeling a little bereft. *Why? Don't be absurd! I'm looking for things that just aren't there.*

It was true, she supposed. Since Adele's disappearance, she'd purposefully avoided going anywhere near girls of her age, whatever that age may have been over the years. But being confronted by a little girl who she thought looked like Adele had been a blow she hadn't expected, and it knocked her sideways for a moment or two. So much so that she was drawn to the girl. "I'm sorry, Emmy, would you mind if I head back home now? I have a headache coming on."

Emmy's eyes narrowed as if she didn't believe Debs, but she nodded and smiled after a moment's hesitation. "Of course. You can meet the rest of my tribe another day. I hope you feel better soon. Let me know how you are later, okay?"

"I will, thanks for understanding. Bye everyone, lovely to meet you all."

"Bye, see you soon," Gina shouted after Debs had spun around and upped her pace.

She turned the corner at the top of the road and her heart sank. The little girl was no longer there. *Shit! Shit! Shit!* She scanned the area, but couldn't see her anywhere. *Maybe her mother or father picked her up in the car.*

Disappointment resonated and guided her footsteps. She walked back through the park, her gaze quickly drawn to the children playing on the swings in the adventure play area. She decided to while away a few minutes on the park bench, watching the older children play. Tears misted her eyes when she reflected on the lost opportunity. Why hadn't she listened to her gut and approached the girl? She'd had many regrets over the years but thought this one would rank at the top of the list.

Logan stirred with the noise of the kids' shouting, having fun in the park. Her hand stroked his cheek to soothe him. "There, there, we'll be home soon, little man."

They set off and were home within twenty minutes. Needing something to occupy her mind, Debs decided to cook a full roast dinner with the chicken she'd picked up from the supermarket the day before. After preparing all the vegetables and putting the meat in the oven, she gave Logan an early bath, then sat down with a nice cup of coffee to watch him play with the mobile above him whilst he lay on the furry rug in the lounge. It wasn't long before her mind drifted back to the little girl. *What if... what if she was Adele? It couldn't have been. But... why couldn't it be her? She has to be out there somewhere, right?*

The inner conversation took place over the next thirty minutes and only ended when her mobile rang. "Hello?"

"Debs, it's Emmy. I'm just ringing up to see how you are, lovely."

"Oh, don't worry about me. I'm fine. I took a couple of paracetamol when I got back and my headache went within ten minutes. Sorry to let you down like that."

"Nonsense, you did nothing of the sort. Are you sure you're all right? You know, you seemed a little distant once we reached the school and, dare I say it, when you saw that little girl at the gates."

"Yes, I'm fine," Debs replied, touched by Emmy's concern. "Please don't worry about me, she looked familiar for a moment, that's all. Me being silly, best to ignore me when that happens."

"No way. Look, if you ever need to chat, you know where I am, day or night. I'd hate to be in your situation, the not knowing must drive you nuts at times. Ouch, sorry, I didn't mean that to sound so unkind, it's just a manner of speech, that's all."

"I didn't take it to mean anything else, I promise. I go through phases like this, you're right, the not knowing is the hardest thing I have to live with as a mother." Debs sucked in a large breath and was eager to change the topic because she was desperate not to think about the what-ifs. "Anyway, I loved meeting Gina today. Good luck with being a grandmother of ten in the future."

Emmy cackled. "Jesus, that was bloody news to me, I can tell you. Can you imagine the phone calls I'd be getting when she finds out she can't cope with three or four, let alone ten of the little buggers?"

"It's not that which would concern me, does she have any idea how babies are born? Can you imagine going through childbirth bloody ten times over?"

"Er no, five was more than enough for me. Actually, four was, but then Cilla came along. I knew I should have kept my legs crossed in bed or resorted to wearing my granny style winceyette nighties."

Debs roared. "Oh, God, you do make me laugh. I bet that would have turned Richard off big time, for sure."

"Makes you wonder, looking back over the years, when money was tight in the last century, how people could afford to have such large families, doesn't it?"

Debs took a sip from her drink. "That thought has often crossed my mind. Of course, they didn't have the benefit payments to latch on to back then either. It must have been horrendous."

"Wait a minute, I think my Nan was one of eight. Now I think about it, she used to sit me down and tell me how they were forced to have bread and jam for dinner some days because Granddad worked as a miner and money was really tight. Of course, they had to sit down and watch him consume a hearty meal to keep his strength up for his role as breadwinner."

"Horrendous times. I know we always like to complain how badly off we are nowadays, but we're not really, are we? Says she with a roast chicken sitting in the oven." Logan giggled and reached for one of his toys.

Emmy laughed. "Yeah, that's true. Hey, lucky you, it's bangers and mash in this house tonight, lump it, luckily my kids love it, so I'm safe there. Bloody hell, a roast dinner mid-week, I hope hubby really appreciates you when he gets home from work."

"I needed something to occupy my time when I got back, to stop the brain going into overdrive; therefore, I thought I'd surprise Martin with a nice meal for a change. He'll be shocked when I plate up, I can tell you, it's such a rarity. He'll probably think I'm guilty of something."

"What, like having a hot stud on the side?"

"In my dreams. I don't think I'd ever have the courage to let another man see all my stretch marks. Any hot sex would need to take place in a very dark room, I can assure you."

"You're a scream. I'm sure most men would be up for that, given the opportunity."

"They might, but I couldn't bring myself to do it, not after what happened with Martin."

"Shit, me and my big mouth, I didn't even think about that. What a bitch I am, sorry, love. Please forgive me? My mind switches gear all the time and then my mouth runs away with me and that's the consequence."

"Hush now. You're blowing things out of all proportion."

"You're a gem. Most women would have hung up on me and never spoken to me again, if I'd brought up having an affair in a conversation. I'm such an irresponsible ditsy mare."

Debs smiled. The more she got to know Emmy, the more she thought how cool she was. "Stop it, you're nothing of the sort. End of conversation, okay?"

"If you insist. I'd better fly, the kids are swarming into the kitchen, so it must be nearly dinnertime. Sending love your way. Ring me if you need to chat."

"I will. And Emmy, thanks for being a terrific friend."

"Get outta here. Enjoy your roast dinner and your evening. What time will Martin be home?"

"Just after eight, like normal, I hope."

"Put your feet up before he comes home then, that's an order, Missus."

"I will. See you soon. Thanks for checking up on me."

"That's what friends do for each other, just you remember that."

Debs smiled and ended the call. She'd found an absolute angel in Emmy. As Emmy had suggested, she sat and put her feet up for the next couple of hours, pausing the romcom she'd selected on Netflix now and again to check on the progress of the dinner. Then she put Logan to bed, relieved that he appeared to be more settled now that they were attending the club.

Martin walked in the front door and wandered into the kitchen. He gathered her in his strong arms and gave her a kiss that left her breathless. "Wow, what did I do to deserve that?"

"It's been a long, laborious day and having you to come home to puts life back into perspective, that's all. How's Logan been today?"

She smiled up at him, appreciating how much he cherished her. "One of his better days. Dinner is almost ready."

He lifted his nose up in the air and glanced around for any clues which she'd purposely kept hidden. "What have we got? It smells delicious."

"Let's hope you're not disappointed. You've got five minutes to get changed."

He swooped and kissed her lightly on the mouth. "I'm on it."

She waited until he left the room and then opened the oven. A satisfied grin spread across her warm face. Everything had turned out just as she'd hoped it would. There was a time in the past, when they'd first got married and she was working full-time, that she'd found cooking the evening meal to be such a chore. Often dishing up burnt offerings when she got her timings all wrong.

She carved the breast of the chicken and put three slices on each plate, then strained the cabbage and carrots and placed them in a glass dish. Then she went back to the oven to retrieve the roast tatties and Yorkshire puds she'd found in the freezer, courtesy of Aunt Bessie. Everything was dished up in all its finery, decorating the kitchen table before Martin entered the room. She watched him pause in the doorway, look at the table and then turn his attention on her.

"Blimey, you have been busy. It's not our anniversary, is it?"

"No. Hey, don't say it like that, as though I never make a decent meal for you."

He crossed the room and bent to kiss her. "I would never say that.

147

This is amazing. You must admit, not something we generally indulge in mid-week, so why today?"

Debs shrugged. "I just wanted to show you how much you mean to me and how much I love you."

He kissed her again, a long, deep, searching kiss. "Let's eat, I'm famished. I appreciate your effort, Debs, I truly do."

"I know. It's good to hear. Now you can tell me about the kind of day you've had."

"Nah, I'll pass on that one. I'd rather listen to how your day has been and don't tell me you've been slaving over a hot stove all day long, that would really upset me."

They took their seats and helped themselves to the veg. Debs took the time to mull over what to say next, but no matter how hard she tried, the right words failed to form in her mouth.

"Everything all right, Debs?" Martin prompted, frowning when she didn't answer his question.

"Yes, just concentrating on dishing up."

He tucked into his meal and sipped at the glass of orange juice she'd put out. "So, how did the club go today? Wait, weren't you supposed to be visiting that friend of yours for afternoon tea?"

"Oh yes, we had a lovely afternoon and then I went with Emmy to pick up her daughter from the primary school."

"That was nice. What was her daughter like? How old is she?"

Debs took a sip from her drink and replaced it on the table. "She's called Gina and she's ten. Bloody impeccable manners, too. Lovely girl and she clearly adores her little sister, Cilla, who is three."

He finished what was in his mouth and washed it down with some of his drink. "It must be nice when kids get along like that."

"I should think it makes life a lot easier, especially when there are five children in the house."

"Crikey, not sure I could cope with that many, could you?"

"No, sometimes…" She inhaled a large breath and rested her knife and fork on the edge of her plate. He studied her. "Sometimes I wonder what life would be like if Adele was still with us."

He covered her hand with his and wiped his mouth on his serviette with his other. "You're not alone there. I know we try to avoid the subject as much as possible, but a day doesn't go by when I don't think of her, what about you?"

"Morning, noon and night, hon. Some days are easier than others. It helps being preoccupied with Logan the majority of the time, but there are moments when I find myself thinking what if."

"It's tough, there's no denying that, sweetheart. I'm glad it's not tearing us apart as much as it did back in the beginning. I don't think either of us could have withstood that amount of pressure for too long. I know it hit you harder in the long term and you still have bouts of depression, which breaks my heart, but basically we've grown to accept the inevitable, haven't we?"

Yes, but what if she came back to us? What if the girl I saw today is Adele? I should have stuck around and followed her. Why didn't I do that?

He rubbed his thumb across the back of her hand to gain her attention. "Debs? You've drifted off again."

"I'm sorry. I was reflecting on the trauma we went through back in the day. Not something we'd want to revisit, is it? Which is why I refuse to let Logan out of my sight."

"I can understand that."

They fell silent and continued to eat their meal. Debs struggled with her conscience about whether she should tell Martin or not about the girl. In the end, she decided to leave well alone, for now.

12

*D*ebs tossed and turned all night; every time she closed her eyes, she saw the girl as vividly as if she'd been standing in the room next to her. In the end, rather than disturbing Martin further, she slipped out of the bed. After checking in on Logan, she crept down the stairs and made herself a cup of tea. She sat and drank it on the sofa. Off to the right, on the table by the window, was a small framed photo of Adele. She collected it and studied the photo long and hard, at the same time recollecting the girl's image. A mother knew these things, didn't she? To have a connection with a child that no one else had, not even the father.

The more she compared the photo to the mental image, the more she believed she was right. Her mind went off at a tangent. What if she went to the school, waited outside for the girl to appear and spoke to her? Would she be wrong, trying to assess the situation? Would the child—Susie, was it? Would she be willing to start a conversation with her? What if the girl's parents turned up and caught her chatting with a stranger, would they punish her? She wouldn't want the girl to get into trouble, but the idea that she could be Adele kept prodding her to take action.

Debs saw two, three and four o'clock drag past; eventually, she drifted off to sleep at around four-thirty, clutching the photo to her chest. Martin found her lying on the sofa when he finally came down the stairs at seven-thirty. He knelt down beside her and gently eased the frame out of her hand. Sweeping back her hair, he kissed her gently on the forehead.

She moaned, awaking from the deep sleep that had finally ensnared her. "Oh my, is it that time already?"

"Why are you down here? Couldn't you sleep?"

"No. I didn't want to disturb you, so I decided to come down here instead. Have you looked in on Logan?"

"Yes, he's fast asleep still. Why were you holding Adele's photo?"

Debs shrugged. "Not sure, it seemed a good idea at the time. A source of comfort, it did wonders in the end. I eventually dropped off sometime after four."

"I'm sorry to hear that, sweetheart. Want me to call in sick and look after Logan for the day, so you can have some rest?"

She sat up and threw her legs on the floor. "No. No, don't do that. I'll be fine once I have a shower to revitalise myself."

"I have ten minutes, want to grab one now while I have my breakfast?"

"That would be brilliant. I won't be long." Debs shot upstairs, poked her head into the nursery to find Logan still sleeping, then dived in the shower. When she emerged from the en suite, she heard Logan beginning to stir next door. After throwing on a clean pair of jeans and a jumper, she fetched the little man and took him downstairs. "Thanks so much, Martin. I feel a thousand times better now."

"Good. You look refreshed and as beautiful as ever. I need to go now." He kissed the tip of her nose and then Logan. "Be good for Mummy, won't you, pal?"

"He will. I'm planning on taking him to the park today." She peered out of the kitchen window and caught a glimpse of the sun peeking through the thick clouds.

"They reckon it's going to brighten up later. I envy you. One more crappy day like I had yesterday and... well, I'd rather not say, not with little ears around."

"I wish we could go away somewhere, just the three of us. You need time off to recharge your batteries; you're working longer and longer hours, you can't keep up this pace, love. Not without it affecting your health."

"I'll figure something out. It would be nice if we got away before the summer was over."

"Want me to pick up some brochures while I'm out and about?"

"No harm in looking, I suppose." He kissed them both again and swooped to pick up his briefcase. "I'll give you a ring at lunchtime to see how you're doing. Try and get some rest, if Logan will let you."

"I think sod's law will come into play with that one. Have a good day."

She walked him to the door and waved him off, then put her plan into action. After tucking Logan into his pram, she togged herself up in a thin jacket to ward off the morning chill, if there was one, and slipped on her trainers. It was only ten to eight, but by the time she arrived, the kids would be going into school; at least, she hoped they would. All she wanted, no, needed, was to catch a slight glimpse of the little girl to make her day.

It took almost thirty minutes to walk to the school; her prediction was correct. Dozens of children had arrived already. Her heart twitched a little. *Oh no, what if I've missed her? No, think positively. I've got this, everything is coming good for me, for us, now; any negativity at this point will prove detrimental.*

The uniformed children filtered through the gates, their parents kissing them and waving them off. Although, there were a few children who arrived unchaperoned. *What if one of them was abducted, what would happen to the parents then? Would guilt play a part in their lives, like it has in mine over the years? Although I have nothing to feel guilty about as Adele went missing on Martin's watch.*

She stood just beyond the lollipop lady, tending to her flock, and studied every child as they passed, focusing on all the little girls. But the girl named Susie wasn't there. Debs remained in the same position until the final child entered the gates and the school bell rang. Still, there was no sign of the little girl. *She must have been dropped off earlier, before I got here.*

Disheartened, and with Logan crying through boredom, she reluctantly turned and walked away from the school. Now and again, she glanced over her shoulder, just in case Susie was late. Before she reached the end of the road, she took one final look and saw a blue car open its door to let a child out. It was her.

What the fuck? That car was parked in the same spot all the time I was down that way. She stood there, staring at the vehicle which was heading her way. Inside the car was a blonde woman who stared ahead of her as she drove past.

Debs was livid. *There's something fishy going on here and I intend to find out what it is.* Her mind wouldn't stop thrashing about ideas all the way home, even with a brief diversion of taking Logan to the park. *Who is the woman? Could Susie really be Adele?*

The questions led to more uncertainty. There was no way she could run this past Martin, not yet, not without more proof. She was caught in limbo with no one to turn to. If she rang the police, they'd probably think she was crazy.

Hell on a stick! What do I do now? What if Susie is Adele? How do I go about proving it and getting her back? What if I'm wrong and my mind is playing tricks on me? What then? Am I losing the plot? I don't know. I'm caught between a rock and a hard place with no way out!

She inhaled and exhaled a few deep breaths, made herself a cup of coffee and then settled down on the floor to play with Logan. He was in a much better mood since they returned home; maybe she should take him to the park a few times a day, if this was the effect it had on him.

Throughout the day, her thoughts remained with Susie and the woman who drove past her. Why did she keep Susie in the car until long after the bell had rung? Was it for her benefit? Did the woman know she was there, watching? What if she hadn't known that? What if Susie was Adele and the woman who had abducted her was being extra cautious? What if...? What if...? Nothing but bloody what-ifs toyed with her mind. How the hell was she supposed to cope now, knowing that Susie might be Adele and she was within reach?

*T*he next few days consisted of Debs conducting the same routine, showing up at the school gates to see the same woman drop Susie off after the bell had rung. In the afternoon, Susie was always left waiting at the gates for the woman to turn up.

She decided to pluck up the courage and take the plunge. On the Friday afternoon, after observing the comings and goings of Susie and the woman for a few days, Debs dug deep and put a plan into action. With all the children now gone and only Susie left hugging the gates, she decided it was now or never. "Hello, Susie, do you remember me?"

The girl frowned and her chin disappeared into her chest. "I'm not supposed to talk to strangers."

"Ah, but I'm not a stranger. Cilla introduced us last week, don't you remember?"

Susie's head lifted and their eyes met. Debs had to swallow down the gasp threatening to break out when she saw the scar on the girl's right cheek. The same scar Adele had all those years ago.

"But Mummy said I shouldn't speak to people I don't know."

Holding back the tears, Debs nodded. "Quite right, too. But we've already established that I'm not a stranger. Are you waiting for someone?"

"Mummy, she's late." Susie sighed. "She's always late in the afternoon. I have to wait here for her until she arrives."

"Every day?"

"Yes, Mummy works. Finishes the same time I do, but it takes her a while to collect the car and drive here. She shouldn't be long now."

Debs cast a nervous glance over her shoulder and then turned her attention back to Susie. "That's a shame. What does your mother do, sweetie?" Somehow, she pushed past the word *mother* sticking in her throat.

"She works in a supermarket, ASDA in town."

"On the checkouts?"

"Oh no, she works in the office doing paperwork all day. She tells me she hates it, but until another job comes along, she's stuck."

"That's a shame. What about daddy, where does he work?"

Her head lowered again. "I don't have one of those. He left us years ago. Mummy says I was very young when he went off, he didn't want to know me when I was born." She shrugged. "I don't care, Mummy and I have a lot of fun together."

"Sorry to hear that, sweetheart."

Susie moved tentatively towards the pram and peered in. "He looks so sweet. I wish I had a baby brother or sister to play with, it would be soooo much fun."

Debs fought hard to keep the words from tumbling out of her mouth as her emotions distorted her stomach. *He is your brother. One day you'll get to know him properly.*

Before she had the chance to say anything else, a car screeched to a halt beside them and Susie whispered a brief goodbye and ran towards it. The woman driver glared at Debs, and she actually found herself withering slightly under the woman's scrutiny. Without saying a word, once her daughter was safely belted into the back seat, the car drove off. Taking a piece of Debs' heart with her. *Shit, I have no doubts now. I'm one hundred percent sure Susie is Adele. What do I do now? Who should I tell? Should I tell anyone? Martin will only think I've lost the plot again. But I need to tell someone. Knowing what I do and keeping it a secret will only make the situation more stressful. Shit! Susie is Adele! I want my baby back, but how?*

13

*S*usie is Adele! Susie is Adele! Susie is Adele!

Over the weekend, her thoughts were in turmoil, so much so that Martin kept on at her to go to the doctor's if she wasn't feeling well. She'd brushed off his concerns, stating that running around after Logan had finally taken its toll on her and she was exhausted.

Martin nipped into town on Saturday afternoon and came back with a handful of holiday brochures, the ones he chastised her about, albeit mildly, for forgetting to pick up during the week. They spent Sunday flicking through the brochures and searching the internet to compare the numerous deals each company had on offer.

"I reckon we should give one of the Greek Islands a go, what do you think?"

"Sounds good to me. You choose, I'm not fussed where we go."

In the end, they plumped for a two-week holiday in a villa on the island of Naxos with its vivid blue sea and light sandy beaches. The evening photos in the brochure highlighted the white houses that rose in the hillside, directly behind the picturesque harbour. Her heart felt lighter than it had all week at the prospect of getting away from it all in September—only another couple of months to wait. *Anything could happen until then. Our family could go from three to four, you never know.*

Adele was never far from her thoughts; whether she was doing the washing-up or making the beds in the morning, her daughter's face was there, at the forefront of her weary mind. She announced she was going to bed early on Sunday night, at around eight, not long after she put Logan in his cot.

"Are you sure you're okay, love?" Martin had asked, his legs dangling over the side of the armchair.

"I'm sure. You watch your Star Wars film, it doesn't appeal to me anyway. I'll go to bed and have a quick read instead."

"I'll come up and check on you during the break."

She kissed him on the top of the head. "There's no need. Forget about me and relax, you've been running around after me and Logan all weekend and you're back at work tomorrow."

"You're both worth it. I've enjoyed taking care of you for a change."

"I'll be back to my normal self in the morning, I promise."

"I hope so. I've been worried about you the past few days."

She waved from the doorway. "You're so sweet. What did I ever do to deserve you?"

Debs settled into bed with her romance and flipped through the pages, not taking in anything that she was reading. Maybe Martin was right; perhaps she should ignore the doubts and scenarios flying around in her head and just concentrate on being a loving mum to Logan and a super wife to Martin instead. *If only I could stop all the what-ifs going on in my head.*

She lowered the book and allowed her tired eyes to flutter shut, but it didn't help. There, forefront and centre of her mind's eye, was Adele as a five-year-old, standing alongside Susie, the ten-year-old, both smiling the same smile, giving her the same distant, helpless look.

Feeling sleepy, she switched off the light and turned over. She could do little to prevent her mind running through the pictures of Adele's formative years in vivid technicolour. After a while, Debs managed to drift off to sleep, knowing that her dream would consist of her searching for Adele.

It wasn't long before Susie appeared. She was running along a sandy beach, an excited ten-year-old eager to take a dip in the sea, letting out squeals of delight as the cold water hit her shins. Susie glanced back at her and Martin, her parents, with a serene and happy smile set in place.

Martin came to bed a few hours later, waking her up as he wriggled in beside her, and he hooked an arm around her waist. She moaned and spooned into him. She always felt safe and secure in his arms, aware that he'd learnt from his mistake five years earlier when he'd taken his eye off the ball. By rights, she should have turned her back on him the second she'd heard he'd abandoned Adele in favour of spending time with that other woman's child, but she couldn't; he meant too much to her, always had done.

The following morning, after the best night's sleep she'd had in a week, Debs got up at seven to prepare Martin a fried breakfast as a thank you for looking after her so well over the weekend and allowing her the space she needed to get her head right.

He ate his breakfast with gusto and set off early. She had no plans to go out that morning, but one furtive glance out of the kitchen window changed her mind. She'd have to be an idiot to stay indoors and ignore the beautiful day on show outside. She prepared the pram with everything she would need for Logan and then set off for the park. It was just past nine by the time she got there. They fed the ducks, spent half an hour playing on the swings and then returned home.

Logan was sound asleep when she checked on him, so she decided it would be for the best to leave him in the pram. She poured herself a coffee and sat on the sofa to watch *This Morning*. They had a few interesting articles on the show that helped distract her until the inevitable happened and she fell into a deep sleep, dreaming of Adele, or Susie as she was known now.

The smell woke her, and she began choking on the fumes as panic set in. She shot out of the chair, grabbed Logan out of the pram and ran to the back door. There was no key in the lock. "Where the hell is the damn key?" The smoke was becoming thicker, making it impossible to see. She glanced back through the house and saw the force of the flames ripping through the hallway had become far more intense.

Shit!

What do I do?

Don't panic for starters.

Find the key. It has to be here somewhere. But where?

She ran her hand along the kitchen worktop and knocked something small that was cold to the touch. The key. It bounced onto the floor. "Shit! Where has it gone now?"

Logan's crying was getting worse. She placed him gently on the floor beside her and crawled around, trying to locate the key. When she finally found it, she picked her son up again, inserted the key into the lock and wrenched open the back door. She ran out of the house, coughing as the clear air filled her lungs. "Please, help me!"

Her neighbour, Doreen, called over the fence, "Thank God, you're all right. The fire brigade is on the way, love. How's Logan? Is he okay?"

When she saw Doreen, relief pushed her panic aside. "Thank you so much. I don't know how it happened. I was asleep on the couch and woke up to find the living room full of smoke. My house is on fire and I have no idea how it started." She checked Logan and the panic rose again, affecting her voice.

"Can you make your way around the front, Debs? I'll meet you around there."

"Yes, I'll come round."

She attempted to go back into the house to retrieve Logan's essential bag, but realised how foolish that would be when the heat hit her, forcing her to retreat. Instead, she undid the bolt on the back gate and ran up the alley to the side of the house and out to the front.

There, she saw the scale of the blaze.

"My God, it's rapidly eating through your house. Come on fire brigade, where are you?" Doreen shouted.

The other neighbours came out of their houses to stand in their front gardens and see if she and Logan were all right. They watched the fire spread quickly to Doreen's house next door. Tears blurred Debs' vision. "I'm so sorry, Doreen. I didn't do this, I promise."

Doreen threw an arm around her shoulder and almost choked on her own tears. "It's all right, Debs, I'm not blaming you. What about Martin? I take it he'd already gone to work."

"Yes, oh my goodness, I should call him, but my mobile is in the house. I didn't get a chance to grab it."

"It's okay. I have mine here. Want me to ring him for you?"

"Would you? I can't remember the number, it's Matlock Imports."

Doreen input the information into the search engine and then dialled the number. "Yes, Martin Jenkins please, it's urgent. I'm Doreen Abbott, his neighbour." There was a slight pause. "Martin, oh my, you need to come home. There's a fire, and the house has gone up. No, they're safe. Debs asked me to ring you... Okay, I'll tell her.... Drive carefully." She ended the call and smiled at Debs. "He's on his way, dear."

"Thank God." Debs strained her ear and could just pick out the sound of the sirens in the distance.

The sobs came then.

She hugged Logan tightly, pushing away the thoughts of what might have happened to them both if she hadn't woken up in time and the smoke had rendered her unconscious.

How did the fire start? It seemed to be in the hallway. I don't recall anything flammable being out there.

Two fire engines pulled up. The man in charge shouted orders for his team to follow and then approached Debs and Doreen. "Ladies, I take it these two properties are yours, am I correct?"

"You are." Doreen pointed to Debs' house. "The fire started next door at Debs' and spread to mine. Please, hurry, it's all we've got. Don't let the fires get any worse."

"We're on it, don't worry. We'll have the fire out in no time at all." He turned away and shouted, "Hurry it up, guys, what are you waiting for?"

Within seconds, two men carrying large hoses whooshed past them and gave the signal to turn on the water. The process took less than an hour to complete from start to finish. Halfway through, Martin arrived and gathered her in his arms.

"What happened, Debs?" They were standing on the opposite side of the road; most of the neighbours had come out to gawp at the blaze.

She shook her head as the shock took hold. "I don't know. I was asleep on the sofa. It looked like it started in the hallway, but I didn't wait around to check out the facts. I just got Logan out of there. We had to come out the back way. Doreen rang the fire brigade. Oh God, I'm so glad we're all still here. It affected Doreen's house as well, I feel so guilty about that."

Doreen walked closer and patted her on the back. "Don't worry about me, dear. I got out, the damage done to mine was minimal by comparison."

Martin stared at the house which had collapsed on one corner, the corner where Logan's bedroom was situated. "God, I'd say you both had a very lucky escape, Debs. That's Logan's bedroom right there."

The fireman in charge approached them. "Hi, just to let you know I've arranged for the Fire Risk Assessment Officer to come over and take a look. You'll need his report when you fill out your insurance claim. I take it you're insured?"

"We are," Martin confirmed. "How did it start, do you know?"

"Once my guys were inside, they thought they could smell petrol. Did you have any petrol heaters in the property, anything similar?"

Debs and Martin stared at each other and shook their heads. "No, nothing. We have gas central heating. I don't understand, we never take petrol into the house."

The fireman inhaled a large breath which inflated his chest. "In that case, the only alternative to consider is that it was a deliberate act."

"What?" Martin shouted.

"It's not unheard of, sir. Someone with a grudge squirting petrol through the letterbox, followed by a lighted match. If that's the case, then I doubt your insurance company will fork out as they'll regard it as arson, might be different if a third party is involved though. You'll need to prepare yourself for a fight ahead of you."

"Gee, thanks for the positive spin on things," Martin replied, shaking his head.

The fireman shrugged and walked away.

Debs jostled Logan on her hip. "He can't mean that, Martin, can he?"

Doreen cleared her throat and said, "Oh, he can. A friend of mine and her son went through the same thing. He had a gang of thugs causing mischief in his street, he tackled them, and they shoved petrol through the damned letterbox."

Debs gulped. "Don't tell me anyone was hurt, please."

Doreen nodded and then bowed her head. "They were. Two of their kids were upstairs asleep at the time. They perished in the blaze. So Martin is right about one thing: you were bloody lucky to get out of there."

Debs clung to Martin's hand. "Don't think about what might have been, Debs, it won't do any good. Jesus, to think this could have been caused deliberately…"

"I don't want to think about that. We need to ring the police."

Martin jabbed a thumb over his shoulder. "They've just arrived. I'll go and see them. Stay here."

"She'll be safe with me," Doreen assured him.

Debs was in a daze. Her eyes were drawn to the damage her beautiful house had suffered, and the tears began to fall once more. She hugged Logan tighter. "I can't believe it's all gone. Who would do such a terrible thing? Why? What harm have we ever done to make someone want to hurt us in this way?"

"It might be gang related, sweetheart. Try not to make yourself worse by thinking about it."

"That's going to be impossible, Doreen. I'm so sorry you're affected by this as well. Can you stay with your family?"

"Yes, don't you go worrying yourself about me. What about you? Where will the three of you go?"

"I don't know. Martin's mother and sister live in the area, but we're not really on speaking terms with them."

"I'm sorry, I had no idea."

Debs shrugged and glanced over at her husband. "We never discuss it. I suppose we're going to have to stay in a B&B or hotel for the time being."

"There are a few nice ones in the area. I'd offer you a room with me, but there'd be no point, obviously."

"The thought was there, though, I appreciate it, Doreen."

Martin walked back with two uniformed officers in tow. "They're going to need to take a statement from you, love. Are you up to it?"

"Oh, right. Umm... I think so, not that I'll be able to tell them much."

Martin slung an arm around her shoulders. "Just do your best. I'm going to try and sort out some alternative accommodation and ring the insurance company, see what they have to say about things."

"Okay."

The officers asked Debs to accompany them back to the car and went through the statement with her. "Is there anything you can add?" the female officer asked.

"I'm sorry, that's all I can tell you. Maybe one of the neighbours saw someone near the house before the fire took hold."

"We'll be canvassing the area, don't you worry about that, Mrs Jenkins. You're free to go back to your husband now," the older male officer informed her.

"Thanks." She left the car with Logan and returned to her husband.

Martin was shouting at someone over the phone. "This is ridiculous. After the amount I've paid you over the years and this is the way you bloody treat me... That's as maybe, but where are you when we need you the most. None of this is our fault and yet you're sitting there in your cosy office, treating us like bloody criminals. You're an utter disgrace. I regret ever doing bloody business with you in the first place... yes, and good day to you, too." He jabbed the *End Call* button and paced the lawn at the front of what used to be their family home.

"I take it they're not going to help?" Debs asked tentatively.

"Nope. Sodding morons. As if anyone can prevent bloody arson from happening to their home. I ask you, what do these people want from us?" Martin shook his head. "Anyway, I'll ring my solicitor, see what he can do to help, maybe he'll find something in the contract. Shit! All our paperwork is inside the house, I can't even present the policy for him to look over."

Debs rubbed his arm to try and calm him down. "It's so frustrating. What about accommodation? I suppose they told you to get lost about that, too."

"Yep, they've basically said we're on our own. Good job we have some savings behind us, if we'd booked the holiday yesterday, we would have been in a right pickle."

"Oh, God, that's so true. A holiday is something we can aim for in the future. Why don't you try the B&B around the corner?"

Martin started to walk away. "Sod using the phone, I'll take a wander round there now. Are you all right here for a while? No, here's the car key, sit in the car instead."

"I'm fine. Take the car, you'll be back quicker then."

"If you're sure..." He nodded and trotted over to the car, which he'd parked at an angle alongside one of the fire engines. Debs watched him drive away as another surge of emotions overwhelmed her.

Doreen hugged her and Logan. "Come now, it'll all turn out right in the end, you'll see."

"I don't think it will. Who could have done such a dreadful thing, knowing that we have a baby in the house?"

"That's the sad part. They must be sick, love. Try not think about it. You get yourself settled in the B&B and have a rest."

"If they'll accept us." Debs struggled to shake off the negativity surrounding her.

"No reason for them to turn you down, sweetie. Come on, start believing, there's no point thinking negatively about everything."

"I know. Ignore me. You've been so kind, considering the mess we've put you in."

"Stop that! You've done no such thing. I'm going to ring my son, see if he'll come and pick me up. Will you be all right?"

"Do it. I'll be okay. I have to be, right?"

Doreen smiled and drifted away a few feet to make the call. Logan reached up and gently punched at her face. "Hey, little man. I bet you're hungry, aren't you?" She gripped his wrist loosely and turned to see where she could go to feed him. The police officers were still around, maybe she could use the back of their car rather than wait for Martin to come back. Something caught her eye at the end of the road. She had to shake her head and take another look, just to be sure.

A car she recognised shot off before she could get a closer look at the driver.

My God, it can't be. What the fuck is she doing here? She didn't... she can't be the one who did this. Why?

Debs suddenly became light-headed and leaned on the wall behind to steady herself. Doreen rushed over to assist her. "Debs, are you okay? Is it the shock setting in? Shall I ring Martin?"

Debs wiped her mouth on the sleeve of her jumper. "I think it must be. Martin should be back soon enough. I'll be fine now, don't worry about me. What about your son, is he coming to pick you up?"

"No. He's away with his family at present and told me he'd come back if I needed him. I told him not to bother. So, it looks like I'll be staying at the B&B with you guys."

"Cool. I'm sorry about your son, though."

"Don't be. He has his own life to lead. I'm not one of those mothers who demand a visit every other weekend, putting the fear of God into their children by threatening to leave them out of my will."

"Crikey, you think people are twisted enough to do that?"

"Yep, I have friends who have told me they change their wills more times than they change their underwear. People need to get a life, don't they?"

"They certainly do." Doreen was such a calming influence to talk with that it didn't take Debs long to forget about the car she'd seen driving off. Martin drew up alongside the fire engine again. The fire-fighters were almost ready to set off now and were just putting the last pieces of their equipment back on their trucks.

"How did you get on?" she asked.

"They only had two rooms spare, so I said one would do for the three of us. They can't supply a cot though, unfortunately."

"It doesn't matter, Logan can sleep with us. Hey, Doreen needs a room as well, she was hoping to stay with her son, but he's away with his family."

"I hope he's on his way back."

"No. She told him not to bother."

Martin shook his head, the disbelief evident in his expression. "Families suck at times, don't they?"

"I wouldn't know. I haven't got one," she reminded him, earning herself another hug.

"I'm sorry. That was insensitive of me."

"Talking of which, do you think you ought to ring your mum, let her know what's happened?"

"No, I have to be in the mood to talk to her at the best of times; if I pluck up the courage to ring her and she starts lecturing me, I'm liable to blow my top at her."

"Okay, it was just a suggestion. Anyway, Logan needs feeding, I'll do it in the car."

"Why not wait until we're at the B&B? I'll let the police know where we're going, just in case they need to speak to us."

"Ask them how they're getting on and if they saw anything." Again, she felt guilty about not mentioning either the car she'd seen or her other dilemma about Susie. Was all this linked? In her mind, it had to be.

Where do I go from here? Should I inform the police? Even though they're likely to shoot me down in flames. Ugh, bad analogy in the circumstances. My head's a mess. What if Susie is Adele and this woman knows I'm her mother? Is that why she caused the fire, to keep me at arm's length, away from Susie/Adele?

She was desperate to run the idea past Martin, but knew exactly what his reaction would be. He'd go tearing around to the school and pounce on the woman straight away, and what good would that do for all those concerned? What if she was wrong in her assumption? What then? She could be guilty of ruining Susie's life forever. Could she truly have that on her conscience? No, she couldn't. Which is why she needed to remain shtum about what was going through her head.

Martin returned with good news. "The neighbour on the right, can't remember his name, you know, the old man who walks the little black and white terrier round the block a few times a day." Debs nodded and gestured for him to get on with it. "Well, he said he saw a woman approach the house. She had something in her hand, but he couldn't see what it was. He also said she ran back to her car, sat there a while before she drove off."

"A woman? What did she look like?"

"That's all I've got, sorry. Fuck, the thought of a woman doing this, well, it set my teeth on edge when I heard. What the hell? Who would want to cause us this amount of hardship, Debs?"

She shook her head and stared over to the end of the road where she'd seen the car leaving. "I don't know. Maybe the police will uncover something we're not aware of."

"Shit! I never thought I'd have to deal with them again, not after what we went through last time. You don't think this has anything to do with Adele's disappearance, do you?"

She looked him straight in the eye and shrugged. She hated keeping things from him. "Maybe, but then, why would it after all these years?"

He thumped his thigh. "Clutching at straws, I suppose. Let's get out of here. Every time I look at the damn house, my temper flares and thoughts of doing serious damage to the culprit surface."

"I get that. I have the same feelings running through me. To think we were deliberately targeted by someone is... unsettling, to say the least."

They said farewell to Doreen, who insisted she wanted to stay for a while longer, and drove to The Haven B&B a few streets away. The landlady, Mrs Goode, couldn't do enough for them. She made them a tray of sandwiches, accompanied by freshly baked scones, jam and clotted cream. It was just what they both needed to help lift their spirits.

"See, there are still some good people left in this world," Debs said. She placed Logan in the middle of the bed, and he swiftly fell asleep, leaving her to get on with the task of preparing the scones. All the time she was busy, her mind was thinking up ways of confronting the

woman who had destroyed her home. Halfway through eating the delicious lunch, an idea flickered. "We're going to need some supplies. We
have no clothes, I have nothing for Logan, nappies, toys et cetera. Do
you have to go back to work?"

Martin flung an arm around her shoulder and kissed her temple.
"No. I told Wayne I needed to take a few days off. I can't say he was
thrilled by my request, but that's tough. He'll have to get on and deal
with it. What did you have in mind?"

"I wondered if you'd be prepared to spend some time with Logan
while I whizz around the shops, picking up the essentials we need. I
could get it done and dusted in half the time, if I go alone, with no
baby attached to my hip."

He smiled and nodded. "That's a deal. I'd love to look after Logan,
it's not often I get to do it during the week. Take my credit card and get
what you need on that, we'll sort out the finances later. I'll probably
need to get a loan from the bank soon anyway, if we have to start
over."

"God, really? The thought of being in debt after all these years of
striving to finally have some money in the bank is galling. I won't
spend much, I promise."

"I know you won't."

They ate their food in silence except for the odd moan of content-
ment that slipped from their mouths now and again. After they'd
finished, Debs collected the plates and mugs, kissed Martin goodbye
and took the tray back downstairs to Mrs Goode.

"My, you were hungry. Was it all right for you?" Mrs Goode wore
a pretty apron decorated with different native birds. Her hair was
showing signs of ageing at the side, but she had perfect skin, no noticeable wrinkles, making Debs think she was in her mid-to-late forties.

"I was surprised we ate it all. It was so kind of you to do that for us.
I'm off out now, we have nothing; everything was destroyed in the fire,
so I need to get a few essentials from the shops. Martin's going to look
after Logan while I'm out."

"I'm so sorry you're going through this. Please, if there's anything
I can do to help, just ask. I might have a few toys for the baby in the

lounge, I could get them sanitised for you while you're out, if you want?"

"You're an absolute gem, that would be brilliant, thank you."

"Only happy to help. Now don't you be shy in the future, if you need anything, you just let me know, all right?"

"Thank you, we will." She glanced at her watch and saw that it was almost two-thirty. Enough time to get to the shops for emergency supplies and then... "I must fly."

"See you later. Good luck."

Debs opened the car door and hopped in. The town centre was less than a ten-minute drive away. The traffic was light, which proved to be a blessing; at least something was going her way for a change.

She dashed around the shops, mentally ticking off items from the list stored in her mind. With her list completed, she made her way back to the car and drove to her next destination: St Saviour's Primary School. There, she parked halfway up the road and remained in the car. Susie appeared at the gate and stayed there as usual while all the other children were picked up by their parents. To her, the child seemed downhearted.

Debs watched every car turn into the road with interest and expectation, until the car she'd seen earlier, close to her house, pulled up. Debs noted the time on the dashboard. *She's earlier than normal. Why? Did she have the day off from work? Was that how she'd managed to do the deed and set the fire?* She switched on the engine in preparation to follow the woman. Susie jumped in the back. There was a slight delay while Susie buckled up, Debs presumed, then the car drove off. Debs kept her distance, allowing another car to get between the two vehicles. That worked out brilliantly until the car acting as a shield turned off at the next junction. Debs held back slightly, but the lights up ahead changed to red and she rolled to a stop behind the woman's car. She pretended to be fiddling, distracted by something on the seat next to her in case the woman clocked her in the rear-view mirror.

The lights changed and they both drove off. On this particular stretch of road, there were two more sets of lights. Debs had to put up with the usual scenario—catch one red light, you got lumbered with them all. At the next two red lights, she carried out the same procedure of trying to look busy while she waited. The final set of lights changed to green and they set off again. Debs got the impression that the woman knew she was being followed by now, as her speed had gone up after their final stop. Debs followed the woman out of town and up a country lane. There, the woman put her foot down, forcing Debs to follow her at breakneck speed. *Shit! Are you fucking crazy? You've got a kid on board, my kid!*

The road had several dangerous bends, and the woman's tyres squealed as she took the corner faster than she'd probably anticipated. Debs remained with her, glued to her bumper; she'd come this far, there was no way she could back down now, not with her daughter's safety at stake.

Another corner loomed and again the woman's tyres objected to the speed she was travelling at. This part of the road was particularly winding. A bend to the right and then a sharper one to the left, all the while getting farther and farther away from town. Debs had the impression the woman was intentionally leading her away from the family home. Yet another sharp bend lay ahead of them; Debs braced herself, glad her old car was up to the job in hand.

Half a mile up the road, confronted by yet another dangerous corner, Debs rounded it and slammed on the brakes. The woman hadn't fared well; her car had left the road and was lying in a ditch, the front end embedded into the hedgerow. Debs yanked on the handbrake and shot out of the car. Her main concern lay with the child. Wrenching open the back door, she found Susie staring at the driver who was unconscious, her head grazed and resting on the steering wheel. Susie appeared to be in a daze.

"Are you all right, Susie?" Debs quickly checked her over, looking for any visible injuries—there were none. She sighed with relief and then unfastened the girl's seatbelt.

"Mummy. What about Mummy? Is she going to be all right?"

Debs was caught in two minds. *Do I ring the police? I should, right? But then, if Susie is my daughter, this is my opportunity to take her back. I need to get her to the hospital, get a doctor to check her over. But what about the woman? What if she wakes up and prevents me from taking her?*

She decided to pretend to make the call and then gripped Susie's hand and took her back to her own car. "Hop in. The police are on their way. I need to get you to the hospital."

"No. I want to stay with Mummy. I don't want to go with you. I don't know you. Mummy, Mummy! Wake up, Mummy!"

"Susie, it's okay. I'm going to take care of you. The police told me I had to get you to the hospital. They'll be here soon, I promise you. We need to get you checked over, sweetie."

Susie hesitated, her gaze drawn to the woman's car still lying in an odd position. Guilt ripped through Debs, but it was pushed aside by the need to be reunited with her daughter.

Finally, Susie relented and got in the back of Debs' car. Debs buckled her in and drove past the wreck, keeping a watchful eye on Susie as she drove. The youngster was distraught. Her tears grew into sobs the farther they drove from the crash site. "I want my mummy, she's all I have. Please, go back, we need to help her. She's hurt, please, I don't want to leave her."

"It'll be all right. I'm your friend, sweetheart. I'm only trying to help you. We need to make sure you're all right at the hospital."

"I don't want to go there. All I want is to be with my mummy."

You're with your mummy, sweetheart. I just need to prove it.

"It's all right. We'll go back once the doctor has given you the all-clear, love."

Susie fell silent, apart from the slight sob that escaped her slender body now and then. Debs parked in the hospital car park and helped Susie out of the car. She gripped her hand tightly, in case the girl decided to run off.

"Ouch, you're hurting me."

"I'm sorry. I'm anxious, we need to get you checked out by a doctor ASAP. Come on, it's this way." Debs followed the signs for the Accident and Emergency Department and walked up to the girl sitting at the reception desk.

"Hello, there. How can I help?"

"Yes, you have to help us. My daughter was involved in a car accident, I need someone to check her over."

"Oh no, how awful. What's your daughter's name?"

Debs sensed Susie's gaze on her. "Susie. She's only ten. How long will it take?"

"We're not really busy at the moment, she should be seen fairly soon."

"Mummy, I want my mummy!" Susie said, tears bulging again.

The receptionist frowned a little as if to question what she'd just heard. "I think she bumped her head on the seat. That's why I want her checked out," Debs said quickly.

"No problem. Take a seat. I'll see if one of the doctors can see you immediately."

"Thank you, that would be fantastic. Come on, Susie, let's sit down over here."

"Mummy, I want my mummy."

The receptionist left her desk, and within seconds, a young female doctor appeared. "Hello, I'm Doctor Carlisle. If you'd like to follow me."

Susie hesitated for a second or two. Debs grabbed her hand and held tight, fearing she might bolt.

"What happened?" the doctor asked. She pulled back a curtain and motioned for them to enter the cubicle.

"Mummy, I want my mummy. I don't want to be here," Susie shouted out of the blue.

"Sorry, I don't understand. The receptionist told me this was your daughter. Why is she asking for her mummy?"

"She's confused. I believe she banged her head when the car crashed."

"Yes, Mummy is back at the car. I must go."

Debs slipped into full panic mode. Lying didn't come easily to her. She gulped and then smiled at the doctor. "Please, you have to help me."

"Is this child your daughter or not?"

"Yes, I mean no. Yes, she is."

The doctor crouched and took Susie's hand. "Susie, is this lady your mummy? Tell me the truth."

"No. My mummy is hurt at the car."

The doctor stood and placed Susie behind her. "I don't know who you are or what's going on here, but I'm calling the police. You can fill them in on the details. This child is going to remain with me until they arrive."

"No! You don't understand. Please, don't do this." Debs clawed at the doctor in an attempt to get Susie back, tears of frustration dripping onto her cheeks.

"Security, security. Help me!" the doctor shouted.

Susie bawled and shouted over and over that she wanted her mummy. Debs' world imploded for the second time in her life. *I can't let them take her from me again, I can't.*

She thumped the doctor in the face and grabbed Susie, but the doctor stood firm, refused to back down and clung to the child. Debs was about to hit the doctor again when a hand caught her fist.

"Oh, no you don't. Get here, woman. You dare strike one of our staff. I'm calling the police to deal with you. We have a no-tolerance rule to violence around here. One strike and that's your lot."

"I'm sorry, I didn't mean to hit her. She's trying to take my daughter away from me. Please, don't let her do that, not again." Debs reached out and sank to the floor, her legs rendered useless and collapsing beneath her.

"Get up. The police will be here soon." The security guard, a large black man, hauled Debs to her feet and dragged her against her will to the orange plastic chairs along the far wall. "Stay there. You move again and I won't be held responsible for my actions."

"I'm sorry. I didn't mean for any of this to happen. I want my child, that's all." She watched Susie walk into triage with the doctor. It jarred her insides when her little girl didn't look back. Debs' head sank to her chest in shame. She rested her elbows on her thighs and covered her face and sobbed.

"Ha, tears don't wash with me," the security guy warned. "You think that all you women have to do is turn on the tap and men will fall for it. Let me tell you, I've been married to a manipulative woman for nearly two decades, she could teach you a trick or two. I'm hardened to it now, lady."

"Please, please, she is my daughter. Why won't anyone believe me?" she implored.

"Tell it to the coppers. They should be here soon."

Debs felt lost, dejected and alone. She couldn't even ring Martin because she had no mobile, that had been lost in the fire.

It wasn't long before two uniformed coppers, one male and the other female, showed up. The security guard gave them a rundown of what happened and then took a step back.

Debs squeezed her palms together and pleaded with the officers, "I'm sorry for the upset I've caused, I didn't mean it. All I was doing was trying to protect my daughter. Please believe me."

"What proof do you have that she's your child and why is the girl asking for her mummy, if you say she's your daughter?" one of the officers asked.

"It's a little complicated."

The male officer tutted and shook his head. "I bet it is. Well, we're not going anywhere until we've heard what you have to say, so spit it out."

She racked her brain, which was confused to hell by what had occurred in the past few hours, searching for the name of the detective in charge of Adele's case. "Please help me. Ring Detective... I can't remember his name. He dealt with my daughter's case when she went missing five years ago."

"Name?"

"Bloody hell, I just told you I couldn't remember. Will you ask at the station for me? Or look it up on your system. My daughter's name is Adele Jenkins. That girl in there is Adele, but the woman who snatched her has been raising her as Susie."

"Okay, supposing I believe your cock and bull story, where is the girl's mother now?"

She jabbed a thumb at her chest. "I'm her *mother*," she shouted, exasperated.

The male officer took a few steps back and spoke into his radio while the female officer stood close to Debs. He returned a few minutes later. "You're coming down to the station with us."

Debs shook her head, and it gained momentum the more she shook it. "No, you can't do this. I've done nothing wrong."

"Either you come quietly or I'll be forced to slap the cuffs on you, what's it to be?"

"No. Please. Let me explain," Debs pleaded. Although by the stubborn expression on the male officer's face, it didn't take her long to come to the conclusion that her pleas were going to fall on deaf ears.

They placed her in the back of the patrol car. Debs glanced over her shoulder as Susie was led away in a second police car which had also turned up. "Where are they taking her?"

The male officer glared at her through the rear-view mirror. "That's none of your concern."

"She's my frigging daughter. I need to know. My husband... yes, call him, he'll tell you the truth."

Both officers ignored her until they arrived at the police station. The male officer opened the door and ordered her to get out. With a heavy heart, Debs left the car and walked into the station with an officer on either side of her, ensuring she couldn't escape.

DI Lance Cooper was waiting for them in the reception area. Debs let out a relieved sigh. "Thank God, you're here. Tell them they've made a grave mistake. I found her. She was here all along."

He held up a hand, forcing her to stop talking. Debs frowned. "Wait until we're in the interview room."

"What? We're wasting time. Where is Adele, Susie?"

"She's with Social Services until we can get to the bottom of all this, Mrs Jenkins." His tone was off-hand which confused Debs even more.

She kept quiet until they were alone together in the interview room. "Thank God you're still here after all these years. I have a lot to tell you, it all kicked off about a week ago."

Again, he shoved a hand in her face to stop her. "Wait until my partner arrives. We'll conduct the interview under caution and will record it. She's just gone to fetch the duty solicitor."

"What? Why? I don't need a bloody solicitor. I can't believe you're doing this to me. After all my husband and I have been through over the years. What gives you the right to treat me this way?"

"The law is on my side, I think you'll find, Mrs Jenkins."

"I beg to differ. The law is firmly on *my* side, if you take the trouble to listen to what I have to say. Why am I being treated like a criminal here? Have the decency to answer that for me."

"All in good time."

The door opened and in walked DS Dorning. With her, she had a young woman wearing a striped grey suit. The solicitor's hair was scooped back to make her look austere and professional.

The sergeant and the solicitor took their seats. Debs was still in a state of shock as Dorning announced to the recording who was in the room and why they were there to the recording.

Then DI Cooper began firing questions at her. "Maybe you'd like to tell us why you felt the necessity to kidnap a little girl called Susie today, Mrs Jenkins?"

"What? I didn't. She was in a car accident. All I did was take her to the hospital to get checked over."

"I see. How were you aware of the accident?"

Debs' brow furrowed. "Because I was following the car at the time."

"And why was that?" Cooper tapped his pen on the desk.

Debs clenched her hands together until the knuckles turned white. "Because I had reason to believe Susie is my daughter."

The detectives glanced at each other, both cocking an eyebrow before Cooper turned back to face her. "So you thought the best way to go about proving it was to kidnap her? An eye for an eye?"

"No. It wasn't like that at all. My mothering instinct kicked in. Susie, or Adele, was hurt, all I wanted was to get her to the hospital."

"Why didn't you call an ambulance for her mother?"

"Would you?" she snapped. "If that woman had stolen your child?"

Cooper's eyes seared her soul and she shuddered. "You caused a crash and left a woman to die."

Debs shook her head. "Don't tell me she died. I couldn't bear the thought of her leaving this earth without getting punished for what she did. For the damage she's caused to me and my husband."

"You're extremely fortunate, she didn't die. Her injuries are bad enough for her to need to stay in hospital for a few days. However, you should have called the ambulance and the police, for that matter. I'd say your motive was obvious from the outset, wouldn't you, Mrs Jenkins?"

"Oh yes, I would. I was desperate to get my daughter back and now you've stolen her from me again and are intent on accusing me of all sorts. Have some heart, for God's sake. No, why should you, you gave up on us, on Adele, years ago, didn't you?"

"That's not true, Mrs Jenkins. Adele's case has always been open, we never closed it."

"Really? You could have fooled me. For the recording, I want you to tell me when you last came to my house and gave me and my husband an update on our abducted child."

He shifted uncomfortably in his chair and the colour rose in his cheeks. "I believe that was nearly five years ago."

"That's right, and nothing, absolutely zilch from you since, and you wonder why I had to take things into my own hands, after the day we've had."

Cooper's head tilted. "Meaning?"

"Meaning, that woman, the one you went to great lengths to tell me I left for dead… it's because of her that my family are holed up in a B&B at the moment." She swallowed down the tears, determined not to crumble until all the truth was exposed.

"I don't understand. Enlighten me, if you will?"

"Earlier today, I was in the house with my baby, yes, I have another child, he's called Logan who is nearly four months old and probably missing his mother like crazy right now, especially after the trauma we both experienced today."

"Can you stop going around the houses and get to the point, Mrs Jenkins?"

"My son and I were having a nap when we were woken by smoke filling our home. Another ten minutes or so and we might have died in the fire. As it happened, I had my wits about me and managed to escape with Logan. The police arrived along with the fire brigade, of course. The fireman in charge asked if I'd had any petrol in the house. I told him I hadn't and asked why he wanted to know that. He went on to tell me that an accelerant had been used and his men thought they had smelt petrol in the hallway."

"I see, so you're telling me you believe this was arson?" Cooper asked, his eyes narrowing as if he was unsure whether to believe her or not.

"I am, most definitely. The fireman will also attest to it being arson, if you want to chase it up. Anyway, I surveyed the area not long after I'd made my escape and saw a car leaving the scene. I recognised the car as belonging to the, shall we call her 'my daughter's abductor' for want of a better name for her? I went to St Saviour's School, that's the primary school Susie or Adele attends and waited for the woman to show up."

"With the intention of confronting her about the fire?"

"Yes and no. I got to thinking today, while sitting in a strange room at the B&B instead of my home, the home I cherished, about who could possibly want to harm me and my child. Seeing that woman's car at the scene only reinforced things in my mind. I left Logan with my husband, I drove into town shopping for essentials as we have nothing after all our belongings were destroyed in the fire, because of that woman's evil, vindictive behaviour to rob me of another child in whichever way possible she could bloody think of." She ran out of breath and inhaled heavily to reinflate her lungs. "I went to the school to wait for the woman. Then I decided to follow her instead. I had every intention of coming to the police, once I knew where the woman was heading."

"Okay, so how did the accident occur? Did you force her off the road?"

"No, I most certainly did not. I would never do such a thing, not with my daughter in the car. That woman tried to flee, she spotted me following her and she put my daughter's life in danger in her determination to get away from me."

Cooper folded his arms and looked thoughtful. "You should have contacted the police with your theory or assumptions."

She sat back, folded her arms and demanded, "And how would you have treated the news? Come on, be honest with me."

"We would have interviewed the woman and put your theory to her."

"And if she'd denied everything outright, you would have accepted it as the truth, without delving into the facts, am I right?"

"No. I'm sorry you don't have much confidence in us, in me, Mrs Jenkins, but I have to tell you, you've gone about this the wrong way. The child in question is now petrified, so afraid she's shut down and is refusing to talk to anyone."

Debs hung her head in shame for a moment and then looked him in the eye. "I'm sorry about that. All I was trying to do was get her the help she needed after that woman crashed the car and endangered her life. This is all *her* fault, she set my house on fire, five years after kidnapping my child, and I'm the one sitting in the police station, being cautioned for my damn actions. All I'm trying to do is get to the truth." She clicked her fingers. "Do a DNA test on Susie or Adele. That's the only way you're going to believe me, I can tell."

His stare was cold and accusing. "Oh, we'll be actioning that all right, don't you worry. First though, I have another question for you."

"All right, I have nothing to hide. I've been honest and open with you so far."

"Good, I'm glad to hear it. How did you learn about this child and what makes you think she's Adele, after she's been missing five years?"

"That's easy. I started at a Mother and Toddler club and got friendly with a woman there, Emmy. She invited me around for afternoon tea, we get on great. One day last week, she asked me to go with her to pick up her ten-year-old child. That's when I spotted Adele, standing at the gate. I was drawn to her immediately, call it mother's intuition if you like. Emmy's daughter introduced her as Susie. When I got up close to her, I realised she had a scar on her right cheek, in exactly the same spot as Adele had one. Since that day, I've been turning up at the school gates regularly. She looks so sad. The woman she believes is her mother is always late picking her up. I struck up a conversation with the girl. She told me her mother works in a super-market and her shift ends at the same time school finishes, but that she has to travel to get to the school to pick Susie up."

"So you felt responsible for her and went to the school to be with her until her mother arrived, is that what you're telling me?"

"I suppose. I didn't know what to do. I had no one I could speak to about my dilemma."

"Wait, you said your husband was at the B&B with your baby, why didn't you speak to him?"

"Martin, yes, I've often thought the same. Believe me, I've been tempted to several times, but chickened out at the last moment. He works hard, extremely long hours. He doesn't want to come home and be confronted by my off-the-wall theories in the evening."

"You admit how bizarre all this sounds then?"

"Of course I bloody do. That was until today. Until that woman torched my damn house. Now I'm confident that Adele is mine."

Cooper inhaled a large breath and made some notes on his A4 legal pad, as did the solicitor. It was the solicitor who broke the silence in the room.

"I don't think Mrs Jenkins' theory sounds unreasonable, do you, Inspector? There's a simple solution here, get a DNA test done. Plus, you need to question this woman. How is she, by the way?"

"She is in hospital with concussion at the moment, no broken bones, which is a relief. But let's not dismiss the fact that Mrs Jenkins here had a responsibility to inform the authorities about the crash in the first place."

"I get that, Inspector. However, in light of what she's told you, surely you can understand her reasons for the way things have unfolded. I suggest you let my client go, as you really have nothing on her, as such, apart from leaving the scene of an accident. Then I would further suggest you question the girl's mother as to the authenticity of Mrs Jenkins' claims. It all sounds very plausible from where I'm sitting. Also, she has a right to question your lack of communication over the years, if you're telling us that the case has remained open all this time."

Cooper cleared his throat and sat upright. "It's not as if we had anything to report. The trail was never really hot to begin with. I'm sure Mrs Jenkins would agree with that, yes?"

Debs nodded, reluctantly. "There is nothing stopping you from questioning the woman. If she's a kidnapper, then I had every right taking that child away from her."

Inspector Cooper ignored her claim. "And that's another thing, as well as leaving the scene of an accident, we're quite within our rights to charge you with child abduction."

Debs laughed. "Are you serious? The irony behind your words is bloody preposterous. I didn't abduct her, I took her to the hospital, there's a vast difference, even you have to admit that, Inspector. I have done nothing wrong, whereas the woman, claiming to be this child's mother, has done *everything* wrong, from abducting my little girl to burning down my home. It's she who should be here now, not me." The tears of frustration ran down her cheeks, and she swiped them away as her anger mounted. "Jesus, what more do I have to tell you to convince you that I'm telling the truth? The truth is there for us all to see, please, don't ignore it. My daughter's life could be in danger if this woman believes the net is closing in on her."

"If the little girl is Adele, she's in safe hands. We've arranged for her to remain in the system until we get to the bottom of this."

Hope surfaced and pushed away some of the anger. "Are you saying you believe me?"

"Let's just say that you've raised some valid points throughout this interview that I intend to examine further."

"Therefore, my client is free to go, right, Inspector?" the solicitor said with a smile.

Cooper's eyes narrowed for an instant. "Yes, for the time being.

Give the sergeant here your contact details. I have a lot of leads to follow up on; once my team and I have done that, I'll be in touch. It could take a few days, though."

"I don't care how long it takes as long as Adele is safe and away from that woman."

"She is. Now, I suggest you go back to your husband and make him fully aware of what's gone on."

"I will. Can I be cheeky and ask for a lift back to the hospital to collect my car?"

Cooper smiled briefly. "I'll organise that for you."

"Thank you." She turned to face the solicitor and shook the woman's hand. "And thank you for having the confidence in me to fight my corner."

"I can tell when someone is telling the truth, Mrs Jenkins. I'll leave you my card in case you need to run anything past me. I hope the inspector here does the right thing by you and you get your daughter back very soon."

"I hope so, too."

The sergeant ended the recording and the four of them left the room.

14

*D*ebs entered the B&B with the bags of goodies she'd bought hours before. Her nerves jangling and taut to the point of snapping. Martin welcomed her with a kiss and a hug; he was holding Logan in his arms and rocking him to sleep.

"Hi, I thought you'd got lost. You've been ages."

She placed the bags against the wall on one side of the compact room and motioned for him to sit down. They sat side by side on the bed.

She prepared herself and revealed the truth.

He listened, dumbstruck, shaking his head constantly throughout her revelation.

"What? Why didn't you share this with me earlier, Debs?"

"I couldn't. Please, don't be angry with me. I thought I was doing the right thing. I know you've been concerned about the state of my mental health, I didn't want you to think I'd finally lost the plot."

He gently put Logan on the bed behind them and reached for both of her hands. "I would never think that. After all we've been through together over the years. The way you stood by me, even after learning the truth about Adele's disappearance. Oh, God, could she really be our daughter?"

"I'm sorry to keep you in the dark, I didn't want to build your hopes up, but what happened today changed all of that. The fire, the accident, the fact I had Adele with me for an hour or so before she was taken from me again. I'm confident it's her, Martin. I know in my heart she is our beautiful daughter."

He gathered her in his strong arms and planted kisses all around her face. "This must have been so traumatic for you. You should have told me, I knew you hadn't been sleeping well lately, I put that down to Logan being gripey. I'm such an idiot, I should have recognised the signs."

"Hey, it's not your fault. You've been working all the hours under the sun." She felt relieved he was being so understanding.

"What will happen now? Do the police know who this woman is?"

"If they do, they didn't share the details with me. I suppose we have to trust the inspector will do the right thing. I've asked for a DNA test on the girl. If that comes back positive, then they'll have to hand our daughter back to us."

He smiled and then glanced around the room. "She can't come here. I need to get my arse into gear and find us alternative accommodation. I'll pop out and get a local paper, look through the *houses to let* section. We'll have to rent somewhere for now, until this mess is sorted."

"Ever the practical one. I love you so much, I'm sorry for not being able to confide in you sooner."

"It's all right. I understand your reasons for keeping it to yourself until you were sure it was her. I think I would have done the same in your shoes. Gosh, we have a challenging few days ahead of us now. Do you think I should ring the inspector or leave well alone?"

"I believe it would be wiser not to contact him, not yet. He'll need to do the research and get the DNA test sorted. I left them a sample of my DNA before I came here. God, I can't believe how close we are to getting her back."

"Hang fire on that, missus, nothing is definite. It could all go belly up and turn out to be a genuine mistake."

"It's not. I know it's her, but yes, I agree with you. Let's set this topic aside for now and concentrate on getting our lives back on the right track. Why don't I search the estate agents online rather than waste money on a paper? Most of them have rentals listed as well as houses for sale these days."

"Okay, you do that while I take Logan to the park, give you some peace and quiet, how's that?"

"Sounds great. Don't be gone long, though. I'd like to spend some time with you while we've got the opportunity."

"Half an hour maximum, I promise."

He set off, holding Logan; another thing they would need to replace was her son's pram. Debs opened up the laptop and made a quick detour to her favourite online site to source a pram. She bought one that was a guaranteed next day delivery, then she went about trying to find them somewhere new to live. There were some absolute dives available in the area for the first budget she typed in. There was nothing for it, but to up the budget to over fifteen hundred pounds a month. She whittled the properties down to a couple of possibilities and waited eagerly for Martin to come back. One place in particular caught her attention. It had a pink bedroom and she pictured Adele sitting on the bed doing her homework, and a smaller blue room that she had earmarked for Logan's crib.

The door opened almost twenty minutes later. "Sorry for the delay, Logan was having so much fun watching the ducks at the park, I didn't have it in me to tear him away. How did you get on?"

She angled the screen his way and pointed out the properties she had chosen. "What do you think? I had no idea the rents would be so expensive. I had to go above fifteen hundred to find anything decent."

"Jesus, really? I guess we're not used to paying a mortgage after all these years. It's going to be tough going backwards, isn't it?"

"Needs must. I like this one in particular and it's not far from our house, shell, whatever you want to call it. So the club and park will still be accessible."

"If that's what you want. Why don't you give them a call, see if we can view it now?"

"I can try. What if they can't fit us in today? It's almost five-thirty now, it's pushing it a bit."

"Then tomorrow will have to do. I'll ring Wayne and tell him I need a few extra days off to sort out this shit!"

"It would be nice not having to do everything myself. We still need to buy a lot of things, like clothes and toys for Logan. I only picked up the basics today. Oh, and I ordered a new pram for him, it's coming tomorrow."

"Great news. You have been busy. I'll go in the hall and ring Wayne. You give the estate agent a call and get a viewing pinned down."

"Umm... one problem, I don't have a phone, remember?"

"Sorry, it totally slipped my mind. Here, you make the call first, Wayne can wait." He passed her his mobile, and she quickly dialled the number.

"Jacksons' Properties, how may I help?"

"Hello, sorry to call so late."

"That's okay, we don't close for another half an hour. What can I do for you?" The woman asked, her tone warm and welcoming.

"At least one thing has gone my way today, then. To cut a long story short, we're homeless after a fire broke out in our house and we're in desperate need of alternative accommodation."

"Oh, blimey, that's awful. I do hope no one was injured in the fire."

"We weren't, mercifully, my son and I got out before it had a chance to take hold. My husband and I are staying in a B&B. I looked on your site and you have a three-bedroom detached house in the Carlton area. It's not far from where our house is, and I was wondering if we could view it ASAP."

"We have the keys. I can vouch for the property, it's in beautiful condition. The previous occupiers had to relocate, that's the only reason it has become available. It would make an ideal home for you and your family. What about this evening? Or is that too soon?"

"That would be fantastic, if you don't mind."

"I could meet you at the property at six, how's that?"

"Sounds perfect."

"I'll need to take down your details for the file. Your name?"

"Deborah and Martin Jenkins. We have a four-month-old baby, would that be a problem for the landlord to consider?"

"Not at all. The previous occupants had a two-year-old running around the place, an adorable little girl called Adele, I believe."

The woman's response caught her off-guard. "Oh, that's a lovely name."

"She was the sweetest child. Anyway, back to you. I'll meet you at twenty-five Piccadilly Terrace at six or thereabouts, depending on the traffic at my end."

"That's a date. See you then and thank you for fitting us in so quickly. Oh, I forgot to ask, is it furnished?"

"Yes, good furniture as well, which will be ideal in your circumstances."

"Oh, it just gets better and better. Sorry, what was your name?"

"I'm Katy Fox. See you shortly."

Debs ended the call and handed the mobile back to Martin. "Some good news at last. She's going to show us around the house at six."

"Excellent. I'll just give Wayne a call and then we'll take a slow stroll around there, yes?"

"I agree. No point in us taking the car. I'm excited about this one, not by how much we're going to have to fork out every month on rent, but it would be nice to feel settled so soon after what has taken place, for all our sakes."

Martin smiled, nodded and rang his boss. To their surprise, Wayne was totally understanding and insisted Martin take the rest of the week off to get his family sorted out with suitable accommodation.

Debs changed Logan and then they headed over to the house to meet the agent. Katy was waiting for them when they arrived. The moment Debs walked through the front door, she felt confident it was for them. Katy gave them a whistle-stop tour of the property.

After seeing the size of the three bedrooms upstairs, Martin agreed. "We'll take it," he said, hugging Debs.

Katy beamed. "How wonderful. I hope you'll both, sorry, all three of you will be happy here."

"I'm sure we will." Debs let out a relieved sigh and kissed Martin first and then Logan. *And there's even a bedroom for Adele, for when she comes back.* An ache in her heart dulled her enthusiasm a little, enough to warrant Martin asking if there was something wrong. "No, I'm just content. Happy to have found somewhere acceptable so soon after the blasted fire, so that Logan's life, and ours of course, doesn't suffer too much disruption."

Martin nodded and asked Katy, "When will we be able to move in?"

"If we get on with the paperwork tomorrow, I can finalise things within a few days, after I've checked out your references of course."

"And what are the upfront costs?" Martin asked, ever the money man.

"Ah, yes. Three months' rent plus another month, which will act as security. Is that okay?"

"It'll have to be," Martin replied.

Debs could tell he was doing the maths in his head. "It's fine, sweetheart, I have a few thousand tucked away for emergencies."

His eyebrows shot up. "You have?"

"We'll drop by at around eleven in the morning, if that's good for you, Katy?" Debs said, ignoring her husband's question.

"That's perfect. Have you seen enough for now?"

Debs nodded and held Martin's hand. "Yes. Thanks ever so much for allowing us to view the place tonight, we would have been gutted if we'd missed out on this one."

"It was meant to be. So glad you've had a positive end to what has been a lousy day for you."

Debs couldn't have put it better herself. The four of them left the house together. Katy got in her car and waved farewell. Martin, Debs and Logan took a leisurely walk back through the park. It was a warm evening, and the sun was beginning to turn the sky crimson on the horizon. "The perfect end to a most horrendous day. We should celebrate. How about we pick up a bottle of wine at the off-licence?"

"And a handful of straws, eh? You're forgetting there aren't any glasses in the room."

Debs tucked her arm through his. "Ugh, I had. Never mind, maybe we can stop off and have a drink and something to eat at the pub around the corner. Can we afford that?"

"Well, I think *you* can. Apparently, you have a few thousand tucked away somewhere safe."

She playfully slapped him, and they made their way to the pub. They decided to eat outside at the table close to the river. The sound of the gently running water helped to ease away the stresses of the day for both of them.

"I wonder how the police are getting on," Martin remarked in a hushed voice.

"I was just thinking the same. I suppose we'll find out soon enough. Which reminds me... once we have the keys to the house, I'll ring Cooper, make him aware of our new address. I'm so excited, heartbroken that all our possessions have gone, but this could be a new beginning for all of us, especially if Susie turns out to be Adele. I wish you could see her, you'd be able to tell who she was right away, love."

"It's hard to think of her walking back into our lives after all these years. That's not to say I wouldn't welcome her with open arms, I would, and I will, when the time eventually comes. But on the flip side, our lives are totally different now. Most of them are taken up with looking after Logan. If she came back to us, it would take some time to get used to being a family again, for all of us. This woman, the kidnapper, is the only person she has known for the past five years, that has to count for something in her mind. It could highlight a tricky situation for all of us."

"I hear your reservations and I know you're right, but, surely, she must have some memories of us. We're going to need to work on that, try to bring those memories to the foreground once more. I think we're going to need help, maybe counselling even."

"I'd say that would be a necessity going forward. Let's not think too deeply about this until we know for sure the girl is our daughter, I'd hate for us to get our hopes up."

They ate their burger and chips, both famished after the day's non-stop events, and took a leisurely stroll back to the guest house.

Adele, and the thought of being reunited with her again was a prominent fixture in Debs' mind as she fought to get to sleep.

15

By the end of the following day, Katy had worked wonders for them; and now, here they were, sharing a meal in their new home. Rented or not, it was *theirs*, something they couldn't have imagined having in less than twenty-four hours.

They settled in quickly, not having many possessions to take with them to the new house. It instantly felt like home, which made all the difference to each of them. Logan especially seemed at ease in his new surroundings. Debs couldn't even begin to imagine what must have been going through his little head at this unsettling time.

The day after, Martin went back to work and that gave her more time to get Logan used to his surroundings. After giving him his morning bath, she dressed him, put him in his pram and then set off to the park. He gurgled happily which put a smile on her face, instantly relaxing her. They weren't far from the park when a car pulled up alongside her and a woman tore out of the vehicle to confront her. She didn't recognise the car, but it was a different story where the woman was concerned.

"You! What are you doing here?" Debs demanded, furious that the police hadn't at least arrested the woman by now.

The woman sneered and shouted, "Don't think you can get away with this."

Debs retreated a few steps, terrified the woman was going to harm her baby, or worse, steal him from her, the way she'd stolen Adele all those years before. "I don't know what you're talking about."

"Taking my child like that. How dare you!"

"What? I haven't got *your* child, she's with Social Services until the police get to the bottom of this. Furthermore, I believe, the little girl you call Susie is my daughter, Adele, and you're guilty of abducting her over five years ago from my husband."

The woman took a step forward, her eyes blazing with anger. She curled a lip and snarled, "What a man he is. Good for nothing, except making babies with other women."

Again, Debs retreated another few steps. "What are you saying? You know Martin?"

The woman let out a laugh so demonic it rattled Debs' bones. "Oh yes, intimately."

"What? Who are you?"

"Go home and ask him who Angela Withers is. I'm sure he'll fill you in on all the details."

"I don't recall him ever mentioning you in our twelve years together. I repeat, who are you and how do you know my husband?"

The woman stared around them which sparked a new level of fear to dart through Debs. She clung to the pram handle, no intention of letting it go. All of a sudden, the woman produced a knife from the inside of her jacket.

Debs automatically screamed to draw attention from anyone in the vicinity, but no one came to her assistance. She was all alone, with a mad woman, holding her and her tiny baby hostage with a blade.

Angela's eyes narrowed and she reached out a hand. "Give him to me and you can leave, unhurt."

Debs flung herself over the pram, startling Logan, and he began to cry. "Don't you dare touch my child. Haven't you caused enough damage over the years? I refuse to let you have him. He's all I've got now." Debs placed herself between Angela and the pram.

Angela didn't say a word, she took another menacing step forward, raised the knife above her head and then yelled menacingly in Deb's face. "He's mine. You don't deserve him. I can give him all the love he needs, just like I've given Susie over the years." She slashed the knife several times at Deb's arms and tried to get to her chest, but Debs side-stepped Angela's thrusts.

The cuts she received stung and shocked Debs, but instead of giving up, her determination rose to another level. *I have to save Logan!* "No, don't do this. Help me! Please, someone help me!" she shouted again out of desperation.

Still, no one came to her rescue. Her gut instinct kicked in. She snatched Logan from the pram. Ignoring her injuries, she took off and didn't look back. Debs heard Angela toss the pram aside and run after her. She entered the wrought iron gates of the park and up ahead, she saw two women sitting on a bench, and Debs ran towards them. When she was a few feet away, she screeched, "Please, help me. This woman is trying to snatch my baby. You have to help me."

The women glanced at each other, horrified. One of them withdrew her phone and punched at the keypad. Debs assumed she was calling the police. Relieved, she finally had the courage to turn and face Angela again. Clinging to Logan, she shouted, "The police are on their way. Put the knife down, Angela, let's talk about this."

Angela kept coming, her face contorted with rage, her cheeks enflamed. The two strangers sitting on the bench screamed. The woman who had been in the middle of making the call dropped her phone. The operator could be heard, asking questions.

"Please, help us. A woman is trying to abduct my child. We're at Longdale Park. Send the police," Debs yelled, not knowing if the operator had heard her or not. She took off with Angela close behind her.

The pain from her injuries was noticeable now but she dug deep, refusing to give in, aware of what the consequences would be if she did. Up ahead, she could see the gates to the park which led to the main road. *If I can make it through the gates, maybe I'll have a better chance of getting someone to help me.* She upped her pace, but then, so did Angela. They were a few feet away from the exit now when the sound of the sirens reached her ear. As much as she wanted to stop and collapse into a heap, she ploughed on, her survival gene kicking in.

The gates up ahead seemed so close and yet so far.

"Don't think you can get away from me, bitch," Angela shouted through gritted teeth.

Debs stumbled on a stone. Resilience kicked up a notch, allowing her to keep upright and surging towards the gates. On the other side, a patrol car screeched to a halt. "Please, you have to help me!" she pleaded on a sob.

Two uniformed police ran towards her, their batons in their hands along with a can of pepper spray. One of the officers grabbed Debs' arm, pulling her to one side while the second flew past her towards Angela. Debs' legs gave way beneath her, and she and Logan tumbled to the ground. The officer still had hold of her arm and helped to break her fall.

"You're all right. You're safe now," the officer reassured her.

They watched the other officer tackle Angela. The knife tumbled from Angela's hand swiftly; it slid across the ground and came to a shuddering halt in front of Debs. Relief swept through her now that the danger was over... until Angela spoke again.

In a tearful voice, she pleaded with the officers, "You have to help me, she's stolen my baby. I was running after her, trying to get my baby back."

Debs shook her head in disbelief at the officer standing alongside her. "Don't believe her, this is my child." A thought struck her. "Please, ring the station, get DI Cooper here. He knows me and what this woman is capable of doing. She's lying, Logan is my child."

The officer nodded and spoke into the radio clipped to his shoulder. Within ten minutes, DI Cooper was standing in front of her, and again, relief seeped into every muscle of her pain-filled body.

"Take this woman away, I'll deal with her later." Cooper pointed at Angela, who was instantly cuffed and marched to the patrol car. She fought the officers, her arms flailing violently and her legs kicking out at regular intervals.

Cooper helped Debs to her feet. "Are you okay?"

"I need to go to the hospital. She cut my arms to ribbons."

Cooper examined her injuries and tutted. "Shit, it might not look much but you could lose a lot of blood if we don't get you to hospital ASAP. Can you walk?"

"I'm not sure. I'm exhausted." She attempted to stand but her legs gave way again.

Cooper swept her and Logan up into his arms, and his partner opened the back door of the car. He deposited Debs gently on the back seat, then hopped behind the wheel and drove to the hospital, the siren blaring. "Please, you have to ring Martin. I want him with me."

"I'll do it," DS Dorning said. She placed the call.

Relieved, Debs leaned her head back and then glanced sideways at Logan who was staring up at her from the car seat beside her. He was quiet, and she sensed he was in shock due to the events. *Can babies go into shock? I'm guessing they can.* "How did she know where I was? That's what I want to know. I thought she was in hospital."

"She was. We received a call about half an hour ago, telling us that she'd discharged herself. Then a report came through that she'd stolen a car from a man on crutches at the hospital. I was on my way over to tell you when the control mentioned that assistance was required at this location. I took a punt and followed up on the call, had an inkling the incident might be connected. I'm sorry she's made your life hell over the years, Deborah."

"I'm just glad she didn't get her hands on my baby, snatching one child is bad enough. Does this mean that you believe me now?"

"Sort of. We can't hand the child over yet, if that's what you're asking, not until the DNA comes back. I'll ring the lab, get them to prioritise the results, in light of what's happened. Sergeant, will you do that for me?"

"On it now, boss."

Tears spilled onto Debs' cheeks. The thought of her daughter coming home to her after all this time was almost too much to bear.

. . .

*M*artin arrived at the Accident and Emergency Department a few minutes after they got there. She was eager to tell him what had happened, but the doctors gave her morphine to dull the pain and her words came out slurred.

"Darling, my God. When will this bloody nightmare end?"

"It's ended," Cooper assured them. "We've got the woman in custody now. She can no longer harm your family."

"Good. Who is she?" Martin asked.

Debs reached for his hand. He bent down, and she whispered the name *Angela* in his ear.

Martin stood upright and stared at her, shaking his head. "I'm none the wiser, love. Do you know her? What about from the group you go to? All this seemed to escalate around the time you started attending the group."

Her head fuzzy, it was difficult for Debs to shake it, to dispute what he'd said. He leaned down again and she whispered, "She knows you."

Again, he stood upright and stared down at her. She could tell he was searching his memory for the answer. Suddenly his eyes widened as it dawned on him. "My ex," he said, the air gushing out of his lungs.

"Your ex?" Cooper asked. "Care to fill me in?"

"I lived with a woman called Angela Withers, at least I think that was her name. The relationship fizzled out." He ran a hand through his hair as he thought. "Oh God, I remember why we split up now. She was besotted with kids. Every month we tried and failed to conceive. The pressure was immense, so intense it drove us apart in the end."

"I see. When was this?"

"A few years before I met Debs. Jesus, are you telling me she did this? She abducted our daughter, Adele? Why? How did she manage it? We were on holiday, miles away, for fuck's sake. How did she know where we'd be?"

Cooper shrugged. "That's what we need to find out. Okay, I'm going to leave you two for now. I'll conduct the interview and get back to you if I find out anything of interest."

"What about our daughter?" Martin asked, his voice tinged with hope.

"We're awaiting the DNA results. We've chased them up, so hopefully they'll come through soon. She's safe where she is, out of Angela's clutches; that in itself should put your mind at ease."

The officers left the cubicle. Martin hugged Debs tightly. "I'm sorry to have unknowingly put you through all of this."

"Family together again soon," was all Debs could muster.

"Yes, darling, hopefully."

*D*ebs was released from hospital the next morning and Martin took her and Logan home. He put Debs to bed and went back downstairs to be with his son. They were having a cuddle on the sofa when Cooper and Dorning knocked on the front door.

"Come in." Martin held a finger up to his lips. "Debs is in bed, resting." He led them into the lounge. The officers took a seat, and Martin placed Logan on the rug with some of his toys, then sat on the sofa. "I'm hoping you have some news for me, for us."

"We have. The good news is the DNA results are back and they've confirmed that the little girl in question is indeed Adele."

Martin slammed back in the chair, the wind knocked out of him. He'd hoped the truth would come out, but now it had, he was stunned by the revelation. "Shit! I can't believe it, after all these years."

Cooper smiled. "I'm delighted for you. I can't imagine the ordeal you've both been through during this time."

"Have you questioned Angela?" Martin asked, eager to know what the bitch had to say for herself.

"We have. Umm… this is where things get a little cloudy. Are you aware that Angela is still in contact with a member of your family?"

He frowned and sat forward again. "No. Who?"

"Your mother."

He leapt out of his seat and paced the floor a few times, then dropped back onto the sofa. "Jesus, are you sure?"

"Yes. When I asked her how she knew you had gone to The Lakes for a holiday, she told me that your mother had told her."

"Bloody hell. My mother and I have had a... frosty relationship, I suppose you'd call it, for years. Yes, I remember ringing her, telling her we were going away, but before we went, I don't recall speaking to her again. Which begs the question how did Angela know when we were going to be there?"

"I put that very question to Angela myself. Her response was that she started following you, daily. Saw that you'd left Deborah and started living with another woman."

The news came as a shock. She had stalked him? "Eh? And that was her reason for kidnapping my child?"

"Kind of. Her main motive was envy, she was envious of you. Seeing you with three children and her not being able to have any, 'tied her insides into knots', was how she put it."

"I can't believe what I'm hearing." He retched. "I feel bloody sick. What the hell was going on in that head of hers? Is that what today was about? She intended to kidnap Logan as well?"

"Yes, only this time, her intention was to kill your wife first."

"Unbelievable. She's insane. No, please, don't let her convince a judge of that, she'll get off lightly if she goes down that route, won't she? She needs to be punished for destroying my life like this, our lives. No one can ever comprehend the distress we've been subjected to since Adele was taken. No one."

Cooper sighed. "She'll need to be assessed by a specialist. No matter how that turns out, I doubt if she'll ever walk free again."

"Thank God. Who knows what she could have done, if she'd really put her mind to it?"

Cooper and Dorning both stood to leave. "I'm going to make a phone call to Social Services when I get back to the station and tell them to contact you ASAP with a view to reuniting you with Adele."

"I can't thank you enough. Debs will be over the moon to have our daughter back home. Thank you for believing in us, eventually."

Cooper winced. "Ouch! I guess I asked for that. I'll be in touch soon."

Martin showed them to the door and shook their hands. He walked back into the lounge, swept Logan up into his arms and spun around on the spot. "Hey, little man, your big sister will be coming home soon."

He sat on the sofa and hugged his son as the years of frustration eased from his shoulders.

He sat there and wept.

EPILOGUE

*D*ebs had shelled out on new outfits for all of them. She bought a pretty summer dress for the occasion. Martin was dressed in a crisp navy business suit, and Logan was sporting a cute little sailor suit she'd picked up as a bargain from one of the shops in town. Everyone keen to make a good impression as today was the day Adele was coming home. Nothing could spoil this day for them.

Social Services had warned them that the transition for Adele wouldn't be easy and that patience would be the order of the day in the months ahead. People were free to offer their advice, but none of that mattered to either Debs or Martin. Debs knew that love would conquer all.

They met Adele at the arranged location: the local park. Their little girl found it hard to make eye contact with them. She kept her head low, displaying shyness and the lost soul she had become. Logan turned out to be the ice-breaker they needed to get her to open up and accept Debs and Martin as her parents again.

Adele gelled with her baby brother immediately, and Logan's endless tears seemed to dry up and were replaced by laughter and cute chuckles the day she walked back into their lives.

Watching the children play in their back garden, the day after Adele's arrival, Debs slipped her hand into Martin's and smiled up at him. "I can't believe our family has been reunited. She's slotted back in so well, hasn't she?"

"She has. One day, in the near future, let's hope she trusts us enough to open up and tell us what her life has been like the past five years."

Debs watched her precious daughter and shook her head. "I don't think I want to know. Anyway, what did your mum say when you rang her?"

"I let her have it, didn't hold back either. If it hadn't been for her big mouth, none of this would have happened."

"Oh no, that's a shame, Martin. I don't suppose she meant anything by telling Angela about you. Mothers tend to speak proudly about their children, I'm sure her intentions were good. Maybe you're being a little hard on her."

"I'm not. You're just too forgiving. We're lucky Adele is back with us. If you hadn't seen her at the school gates a few weeks ago, we'd be none the wiser and still missing our beautiful daughter. Who knows when our nightmare might have ended?"

Her emotions soared. She was relieved everything had finally fallen into place and that they could finally get their lives back. "I know. We have to be thankful that someone was looking down on us."

He nodded and hugged her. "She's back now and I know neither one of us is about to let her out of our sight in the future, neither of them, right?"

"Definitely. I don't think I could ever go through dealing with that nightmare all over again. I love you Martin Jenkins, thank you for having always been by my side throughout this horrendous ordeal."

"I love you, too. Hey, why don't we top things off by renewing our vows? I'm sure someone we know will be eager to be a flower girl."

Debs smiled up at him. "That, dear husband, is the best idea you've ever had. I'd love to."

THE END

*T*hank you for reading my latest psychological thriller, maybe you'd like to check out another one here. **I Know The Truth**

*T*he first book in the DI Sam Cobbs detective series which is set in the beautiful Lake District is now available for pre-order, pick up your copy of To Die For here.

*M*aybe you'd also like to try one of my edge-of-your-seat thriller series. Grab the first book in the bestselling Justice here, CRUEL JUSTICE

*O*r the first book in the spin-off Justice Again series, **Gone in Seconds.**

*P*erhaps you'd prefer to try one of my other police procedural series, the DI Kayli Bright series here, **The Missing Children.**

*O*r maybe you'd enjoy the DI Sally Parker series set in Norfolk, UK. **WRONG PLACE.**

*A*lso, why not try my super successful, police procedural series set in Hereford. Find the first book in the DI Sara Ramsey series here. **No Right To Kill.**

. . .

The first book in the gritty HERO series can be found here. **TORN APART**

KEEP IN TOUCH WITH M A COMLEY

Pick up a FREE novella by signing up to my newsletter today.
https://BookHip.com/WBRTGW

BookBub
www.bookbub.com/authors/m-a-comley

Blog
http://melcomley.blogspot.com

Join my special Facebook group to take part in monthly giveaways.

Readers' Group

Made in the USA
Las Vegas, NV
02 September 2021